HURRY UP AND RELAX

Hurry Up and Relax

Nathan Leslie

Washington Writers' Publishing House
Washington, DC

COVER DESIGN by Lou Ann Robinson
BOOK DESIGN and TYPESETTING by Barbara Shaw

Library of Congress Cataloging-in-Publication Data

Names: Leslie, Nathan, 1972- author.
Title: Hurry up and relax / Nathan W Leslie.
Description: Washington, DC : Washington Writers' Publishing House, [2019]
   | Summary: "In these 23 darkly comic short stories, Nathan Leslie
   portrays self-appointed cops, shoplifting teens, gym rats, prayformers,
   polyamorous gamers, Bob-obsessed friend-collectors, hug phobics, online
   stalkers, dinosaur erotica writing gurus, and self-medicating placenta
   eaters. Within these pages you will discover the pressing need to Hurry
   Up and Relax!"— Provided by publisher.
Identifiers: LCCN 2019022669 (print) | LCCN 2019022670 (ebook) | ISBN
   9781941551196 (paperback) | ISBN 9781941551219 (epub)
Classification: LCC PS3612.E78 A6 2019 (print) | LCC PS3612.E78 (ebook) |
   DDC 813/.6—dc23
LC record available at https://lccn.loc.gov/2019022669
LC ebook record available at https://lccn.loc.gov/2019022670

Printed in the United States of America

WASHINGTON WRITERS' PUBLISHING HOUSE
P. O. Box 15271
Washington, D.C. 20003
More information: www.washingtonwriters.org

TABLE OF CONTENTS

Hurry Up and Relax: A HOW-TO GUIDE

For sage advice on how to:

☛ Eat cheesy poofs in a sexy way, see page 125

☛ Befriend a guy named Bob, see page 7

☛ Operate a toll booth during a heat wave, without losing your shit, see page 87

☛ Become your own police force of one, see page 15

☛ Effectively utilize the second person without losing your sense of self-worth, see page 3

☛ Transition from writing respectable literary works to writing (less respected) dinosaur erotica, see page 191

☛ Wet Vac a basement, see page 165

☛ Invent your own fake language, see page 93

☛ Have a meaningful couples weekend away despite the rain, see page 148

☛ Become addicted to the StairMaster, see page 104

☛ Avoid becoming addicted to the StairMaster, see page 118

☛ Learn the relationship between the music of Brian Eno and your shin, see page 50

☛ Make a mean placenta fricassee, see page 186

☛ Speedily initiate the divorce proceedings, see page 144

☛ Attend a social engagement you secretly want to avoid equipped with less-than-perfect edible food items, see page 174

☛ Subsist on orange-colored faux-orange juice, frozen mini-bagels and translucent coffee, see page 79

☛ Steal a two person kayak from a big-box store and get away with it, see page 58

☛ Build a top-tier collection of used celebrity socks, see page 179

☛ Develop a poor professional business model and lose tons of money, see page 157

☛ Deal with fake Norwegian guys named Sven who insist on hugging protocol, see page 36

☛ Cope, if you happen to become a psychotic Internet stalker dude, see page 136

☛ Receive laurels from the United Federation of Touchless Touch Masters, see page 28

☛ Become a better husband/wife/father/mother/son/daughter/sibling, see page 894

☛ Find inner fulfillment, see page 783

☛ Learn how to relax before it's time to stop relaxing, see page 68

ACKNOWLEDGEMENTS

Thank you to the following publications who published the following stories from this collection (in some cases in a slightly different form). *Juked* for "The Collector," *Bull* for "Courting the Un-Bob" and "The Enforcer," *Adirondack Review* for "Drop," *That Literary Review* for "Exact Change," *Decomp* for "Head to Toe," *Gargoyle* for "A Helping Hand," *Painted Bride Quarterly* for "It Can't Hurt, Can It?," *Per Contra* and *Flash! Writing the Very Short Story* by John Dufresne (W.W. Norton) for "The Other Person," *Little Patuxent Review* for "Rule the Day," *Defenestration* for "You are the Product" and *Lake Effect* for "A Friend of the World."

I would like to especially thank Caroline Bock, Kathleen Wheaton and Jake Weber for their help with the manuscript—I am indebted. I would also like to thank Barbara Shaw for the terrific book design and Lou Ann Robinson for the imaginative and wonderful cover. "A Friend of the World" is inspired, in part, by *The Steal: A Cultural History of Shoplifting* by Rachel Shteir. Thank you also to the fine folks who chose this manuscript as the 2019 WWPH prize winning book. As always, thank you to Julie for putting up with me and my ways.

THE OTHER PERSON

YOU WRITE THE STORY in the second person. It's your go-to point of view now. You like its edge, its resonance of irony even if your story lacks said irony (it adds irony). You makes anything possible. You is the new me.

By writing the story in the second person you can avoid concerning yourself with psychological dimensions; you can avoid over-thinking. You makes every sentence glow, you think. It makes the reader the story. It's direct engagement. It's intense. Immediacy.

It's like a camera down the gullet. It's like being inside someone. It's like sex, without the emotional messiness.

Your story is about an anonymous man (or woman perhaps—though most yous are men) who walks through the urban blight, looking for a child named Cass. You had just heard the Mama's and the Papas on the Classics station, and hadn't really thought about Mama Cass for years. Cass? Why not Cass. You like the allusion.

Turntable Hipsters should know.

Fiction should educate. The urban blight is somewhat inspired by the city in which you live, though a far more post-apocalyptic version thereof. Instead of Starbucks and little pastry shops and Thai restaurants with orchids on every table you write about the desiccated skeletons of once productive textile factories, crack vials, and prostitutes with scabs on their faces. You've never seen desiccated textile factories, crack vials or prostitutes (scabs or scab-free), but you use your imagination. If you don't know, *you* will. Zombies, there's always zombies. Second person zombies.

You wonder, Why the post-apocalyptic mélange? In a more or less peaceful age you notice more horrific violence, more dripping pipes and sunless urban canyons. Yet from whence does this come? You know the recent recession hasn't helped, but aren't zombies an overreaction? Are you really living in an urban wasteland? There's a Whole Foods on every other corner. Shit's nice.

Once, just once, you'd like to meet a reader. This would help clarify your purpose. And not a reader-who-is-also-a-writer hawking his latest "fabulist" novella at AWP ("It's like *19Q4*, only shorter, and less, you know, Japanese")—a real reader. One who just reads, doesn't write. Even more ideal would be catching a reader in the middle of reading one of your stories, midstream so to speak. You'd love to ask the reader if he/she felt as if she/he was the protagonist. You'd love to know if she/he was walking through the rat infested heroin streets whilst searching for Cass. And if he/she felt as if he/she could place him/herself in the story, did you feel invested in it? Did you feel the intensity of the *you*? Did you meld with the story? Did the fourth wall come crumbling down?

You keep your eyes peeled. You've published in several small magazines, but you never see people out and about in society reading the *Orange Toad Belly Review* (circulation 250). Even if you positioned yourself on the campus of Southwestern Central Missouri State Community College (South Bend Campus), you doubt you would see people walking around reading the *Orange Toad Belly Review*. They're in a box somewhere in some associate professor's office. Behind some other boxes of other shit he's been meaning to get to.

But then. You're on the Metro people watching through the reflection in the window. Through the reflection you see a young woman scrolling on her I-Pad. She clicks on several literary pages, then—amazingly—clicks on the *Orange Toad Belly Review*. You watch her scanning the page, then she clicks on *your* story.

Ten seconds is a long time, you think. For ten seconds your story, "Gristle and Bone" lingers on her screen. It does more than linger. It pulses. It, like, *throbs* on her screen. She's reading it. You aren't breathing. You are watching her read. A real person, reading.

You hold your breath. For the first time your life you feel as if you are really and truly an author. You feel as if you have a voice and someone wants to hear it. You feel as if you could be the author you've always wanted to be—an amalgam of Pynchon and Vonnegut with a dash of Rushdie and Márquez and a dusting of Barthelme. You feel important.

She utters a quick little snort. Then she clicks away. She clicks to Facebook.

"Wait, wait, wait," you say, startled by the intensity of your reaction. You turn your head.

"Huh?" the reader says.

"Just…why did you click away from that last piece?"

"Are you, like, *spying* on what I'm looking at?"

"No."

"Yes, you are. It's, you know, really none of your business."

"Ordinarily, I'd agree but I wrote that."

"You wrote that?"

"Yeah. So I was wondering. Why did you click away?"

She says she doesn't know. It just didn't *appeal* to her. It was too negative. Too caustic. It didn't have the human dimension she's looking for in a story. It was missing something. Plus the whole "you" thing is weird, isn't it? It feels forced. Am I supposed to *be* that person, or something? I'm not. I'm me. She snorted. *Snorted.*

"I see," you say.

"Sorry," she says, and lowers her head back to her I-Pad. "Gotta be honest."

You wander down the streets of your pleasant urban reality. The craft shops seemed to have tripled in the past three years. You pass three grocery stores in three blocks. Now there's a tea shop. More bagel shoppes than you can count. Aren't those little art galleries precious? You can't help but peek inside one or two crystal shops. Or is that you? You're not sure anymore.

You plop down on your "reclaimed" vintage sofa you bought for $1,687 at Dukents, the new furniture boutique down on 12th Street. It probably cost $100 to make back in 1979, or whatever. Now it's "vintage." Perhaps you should invest in furniture, you think. You close your eyes and breathe and listen to your breathing. It's good to be alive, you think. One day you will write something good. You know you will. You'll keep trying. Your ten seconds will be elongated. You will become loved. We all should, shouldn't we? Isn't that what this is all about?

COURTING THE UN-BOB

THERE ARE BOBS. I am, in fact, surrounded by Bobs. There are so many Bobs I've lost track of the Bobs. I no longer use surnames. I use traits. All these Bobs.

Beer Bob is my go-to Bob, my everyday Bob. He'll drop by and we'll drink a beer. He's also Working Bob—meaning really working, not just farting around on the laptop doing "consulting" or some other glorified horseshit. Most Bobs are involved in horseshit.

I get along with Beer Bob. We have much in common. Like me, Beer Bob is divorced. Like me, Beer Bob tries to muster a sense of hilarity, even if he's occasionally jaundiced. Like me, Beer Bob shambles about (his cane was whittled from the leg bone of an ox). He says the cane is "fortified" to hold up over time. I personally avoid catering to canes, but my gout does, usually, get me pogoing.

If only all Bobs were as easy as Beer Bob.

Craigslist Bob is an angler. He lives two houses down, which creates its own hornet's nest of productions. CL Bob buys stuff primarily off Craigslist, though he also scours rummage sales on Saturday mornings. He makes his living, as it were, re-selling such purchased goods on E-bay. He must be fucking good at it because I can't fathom how anybody can really survive in this manner.

Unfortunately, Card Shark Bob hates Craigslist Bob because of some real or perceived slight (Card Shark Bob won't say). This creates almost constant tension in their midst; Card Shark Bob is a nasty person to offend. That and Card Shark Bob is half the size of Craigslist Bob, so they have a real gnat-and-bull dynamic at work.

For some reason, both Craigslist Bob and Card Shark Bob frequently visit to depict the details of their boring wrangles. This would be fine in and of itself, but Card Shark Bob is awake at some ungodly hour—he usually falls asleep at four-thirty—and Craigslist Bob pops by my house to offer me the latest what's what.

"I don't really have a dog in this fight," I say. "I mean."

Craigslist Bob shrugs and flies loose anyhow.

Complicating this is Barefoot Bob, who lives in my basement. Barefoot Bob is studentesque though he's thirty-one and he only takes one class a semester. Online. He delivers pizza for Jake's Pies one night a week and otherwise day trades stocks for a living. Sort of. So, he's padding about barefoot or glued to his computer screen by the non-operating wood stove positioned next to the non-operating exercise equipment (the stationary bike churns only at "10," which is equivalent to riding up a forty-five degree incline). If Marie was still around, she'd toss the thing in the nearest refuse heap. I'm nostalgic.

Barefoot Bob complicates the mix of Bobs because Barefoot Bob is fucking Craigslist Bob's ex. Craigslist Bob knows this, but isn't supposed to know (Card Shark Bob told him in a demonic act of malevolence). So they both pretend nothing is happening. The good news here is that Craigslist Bob doesn't particularly care because he's sworn off "genital mashing," as he calls it. For good. He cites spiritual slash religious justifications: "I'm a man of the Lord," Craigslist Bob says. "And the Lord doesn't cater to the rough and sordid." And if he said it is, it must be true. Probably is. The tautness is now internalized: I know Craigslist Bob knows but isn't saying—and I'm certainly not (preferring to shy away from skirmishes—unlike the other Bobs who love to sink their hands into the muck).

Aside from the peripheral Bobs in the mix—Bakery Bob, Lunch Bob, Guttersnipe Bob, Taxidermist Bob and Library Card Bob—the last major Bob I should mention is Un-rival Bob, my ex-wife's ex (she remarried again), who befriended me in an act of red-faced guilt, and who, likewise, cannot find common ground with Beer Bob because—in my view—Un-rival Bob is jealous of my off-the-cuff intimacy with Beer Bob. It's unstated, of course, but the problem is there. My imagined conversations go like this:

"Bob."

"Yes, Frank." That's me.

"I don't really like Beer Bob better than you, per se. It's just that he's been around longer. He was here, you know, during…when…"

"Oh, I know. It's okay."

"It's just, he's an older Bob. You're just as relevant. No 'relevant' isn't the best word. You're just as 'able'—there's a better word. Never mind, forget it."

"I know, it's okay."

"I feel guilty."

"*You* feel guilty? *I'm* the one who should feel guilty. I didn't mean— "

"No, it's fine, Bob. She has problems. She needed something new."

"Still does."

"Yup."

Mostly I'm crazy about the Bobs. I revel in my late bachelorhood, as it were. I have zero pressure in my life, zero sense of obligation. The Bobs keep me afloat. Without the Bobs, not good at *all*. I know this.

WHAT HAPPENS is this: I meet Lunch Bob at the Black Beret—a new overly self-conscious café Lunch Bob wanted to try. I have a regular Tuesday thing with Lunch Bob (different restaurants each week), have since '97. That's why he's Lunch Bob. Ritual keeps us ticking.

I can tell right away it's one of these joints that doesn't give you enough to eat. I look at the other tables—they're nibbling at little hand-sized sandwiches, puny salads, tiny saucer-sized plates of veggies or appetizers.

Lunch Bob is on a diet.

We look over the menus and start talking. Lunch Bob likes to tell stories about his "wild youth," which bear no real relevance to anything. He collects these stories and needs to tell them to make them real. So, he's telling this one about going dirt-biking with a serial killer—at least he *thought* the guy was a serial killer. Everybody did. Had the fish eyes and the wacko Manson hair and everything.

We get our food and we're digging in. And here it's important to include a comment about this long-standing tradition: Lunch Bob is the messiest fucking eater I've ever seen. At no point in our relationship has Lunch Bob ever walked out of a restaurant, coffee shop or café with a clean shirt. Usually his pants are soiled. It's like eating lunch with a three-year-old. He's telling this story and even though the Black Beret serves a chintzy little tea cup of soup, a greater portion of the soup spatters all over Lunch Bob's shirt than he actually ingests.

I cannot for the life of me concentrate.

"Bob," I say, interrupting his maniacal childhood dirt bike tale. "Your shirt."

He glances down, looks up at me and shrugs.

"Got another one in the car. Anyway, as I was saying." Of course. He always has the backup shirt.

The stares. I shield my eyes. It looks as though Lunch Bob got in a food fight with the high school rugby team.

So. Fine. Next Tuesday comes around and I call Lunch Bob a few hours prior and cancel (unlike me).

"Sorry, man," I say. "I have this thing today."

"What 'thing'? You haven't missed one of our lunches in four years."

"I know, I know. I have this brutal canker sore. I mean I really can't eat. It stings something terrible. Like a crab clinging to the inside of my face. Like someone is stabbing me in the cheek with the pointy end of a dart."

After a back and forth, he lets me off the hook. Which is perfect because Gary and I want to grab some pizza from that joint in town. Gary is my other roommate, and sometimes he seems about the only guy I know not named Bob. Also, he's relatively "normal," which also explains why I haven't mentioned him until now. But there I am cheating on Bob with the Un-Bob—and nobody could be more Un-Bob than Gary. Unlike the Bobs Gary is 1. Mellow 2. Wise 3. Distant from unnecessary conflict. Gary likes to drift in the background, a kind of male wallflower.

GARY AND I are sliding the two pizzas in the backseat about ready to drive home when Lunch Bob lurches up behind us. And when I say behind us—I mean, he parks his stupid red jeep directly behind my cheap man's compact.

"How's that canker sore feeling, Frank? I hear pizza sauce is terrific for canker sores! Tomato sauce is supposed to be a real balm, a cure-all for canker sores!"

"Bob, these pizzas—"

"Horse. Shit," Bob says. "Jesus, Frank. What happened to us?"

"Can we pull out now?" I say.

For a minute he just sits there moping—and no, we can't pull out.

"Bob!" I say.

"Finally, he peels off into a shady spot under the weeping willow, or something. Gary and I drive home and eat the pizza. Damn good, also.

YES, I DO feel guilty. Not only that, but by invoking another Bob at the scene—I didn't reveal *which* other Bob it was—Lunch Bob is insanely envious and reasons I cheated on him with a Bob (Lunch Bob was unaware of Gary). He must've thought Gary was also a Bob. So then he doesn't call and despite my calls, e-mails and apologetic entreaties, Lunch Bob stiffs me.

Fuck *me.*

Finally, I receive a voice mail from Lunch Bob saying he wants the "other" Bob to come *with* next time so that he can "meet the enemy." In the voice mail, he proclaims my little tête-à-tête with the "other" Bob to be a loogie in the face of "Honor in this world." He proclaims that from now on he insists the "other" Bob come along to our Tuesday lunch hangs lest I deny myself my true urges, which are not done with him, per se, but rather with an alien Bob who I must find less tiresome, less "intense." Less Bob-by.

Well, as a matter of fact....

I call back immediately but it rings through to voice mail.

"Bob, it's me, Frank. Thanks for your message. I can bring one of my other friends named Bob next week for our little lunch, but the guy I got pizza with last week isn't named Bob. That's my roommate, Gary. I've spoken of him before, I believe. In fact, you met him—you just forgot. I was just...I don't know...At any rate, that's just fine."

I mean.

These are *grown men* we are talking about.

Well, Lunch Bob goes ballistic. He writes his ranty e-mail which proclaims "true friendship" a remnant of the past and hopes I can rectify his wounded ego, blah, blah, blah, blah. "If I have the time."

I mistakenly paraphrase all of this to Craigslist Bob and Barefoot Bob one morning at the breakfast bar. We're eating Pop-Tarts and drinking coffee with lots of sugar. My life is asinine.

"Here's what you do," Craigslist Bob says.

ALL OF THIS because Lunch Bob lacks the common sense to eat without dribbling his lunch all over his white and yellow polo shirt at a whimsical café, which will likely go out of business a month from now. Everyone is so *sensitive* these days.

For a few weeks everything calms down. On the surface. I don't hear from Lunch Bob and he doesn't hear from me. On Tuesdays I eat pizza with Gary. That's my replacement routine. Gary is no problem to get along with. One or both of us picks up the pizza. We watch bowling or whatever third-tier sport is on ESPN at lunchtime on a Tuesday. It's easy-peasy.

Craigslist Bob is not one to fuck around. He drives over to Lunch Bob's place and barks at him to get in the damn car—which he does. Then he whisks Lunch Bob back to my place where Barefoot Bob, Beer Bob, Card Shark Bob and some of the other more peripheral Bobs (and Gary) have gathered upon Craigslist Bob's request. He gave them the lowdown. Filed them in.

"Let's straighten this shit out," I can hear Craigslist Bob saying, walking in.

Lunch Bob affixes a sheepish smile on his face (like he doesn't really believe in his expression himself). Does he trust it was he who wrestled Craigslist Bob here (instead of the reverse)? He half shades his eyes from the small crowd—Lunch Bob seems to know the deal.

"I'm very ritualistic," he says. "I've just, you know, I've always liked the comfort they provide."

"Stop blowing smoke," Card Shack Bob says.

"I've been meeting Frank for lunch for many years now. I probably—"

"We don't care," Taxidermist Bob says.

"No, I know. I've overreacted. I can do that."

"Forget all that," Craigslist Bob says. "Which of these guys was there at the pizza place with Frank?"

A lineup of agitators.

Lunch Bob looks everyone over a couple of times and nods Gary's way.

"This guy."

"My name's Gary."

"I thought everyone around here was a damn Bob," Lunch Bob says.

"Not Gary," I say.

"Oh shit, I'm sorry," Lunch Bob says.

"Glass of water?" I ask.

"Sure."

He drinks some. A third of it dribbles down his neck onto his shirt.

"Damn, Bob. Where did you learn how to drink water?"

One of the Bobs said that. Not sure which one.

I STILL SEE the Bobs—can't avoid them. But I've been hanging with Gary more recently. Gary has a simplicity to him which I like. This was one of the problems I had with my ex-wife. She was a good person but she had too much nervous energy. When the chips were down, she'd flip.

Gary convinces me to make a conscious decision to distance myself from all the chaos. "No need for any of it," he says. "You're only retired once."

So, I still meet up with Lunch Bob, but only once a month. He adjusts. I tell Craigslist Bob I'm busy if I don't feel like talking. I don't answer every guilt-stricken e-mail from Un-Rival Bob. Mostly, I try to court the Un-Bob. Well, not courting exactly…

I go outside.

I step away from the computer.

THE ENFORCER

☛

This all started when my doppelgänger up and died. He wasn't an absolute doppelgänger, but he was a near-near doppelgänger. My name is Ned Leaven. His name was Ned Leavan. We looked almost exactly the same, like two identical twins ripped from the same womb. Sandy hair, short, a thicket of back hair, chlorine eyes, small pupils, red in the face, tiny little corn kernel teeth, unhealthy amounts of gingivitis as a result of tiny contact points. I mean, the guy was my age, a couple months younger in fact.

What happened was this: broadsided on the Beltway, sunny-blue-skied-day, middle of the afternoon. You'd think it was a drunk, some SUV Beemer, some rich guy texting his eighteen-year-old mistress. Nope. Pen pusher fell asleep at the wheel on his way home from work—allergy medicine or some such. Crash, boom, bam. Over for Mr. Ned Leavan. Father of two. Lived one point two six miles away. Just like me, minus the internal stuff (which nobody really cares about, let's be honest).

So what did I do? I sent the usual—flowers and a note of commiseration and pity, but what can you really do or say in such a situation? Nothing. I signed the card "Ned"—only "Ned"—so as to not dredge up reminders for the mourning family. I didn't dare breathe a mention of the fact that I looked *exactly* like dead Ned.

At the time, I was unemployed—about eight or nine months of

15

that caca, actually. Received the pink slip (it wasn't pink, and it wasn't a slip) from the contractor. Kaput. Seventeen years and say-o-nora. My life was watching *Judge Judy*. Doing errands for Wifey at one in the afternoon. It wasn't emasculating exactly—it was just dull. I was bored out of my freaking gourd. And it was, probably, a wee bit emasculating, also. At forty-nine, Einstein was Einstein. Ford was building cars and anti-Semitism. Disney was up to his elbows in Mickey Mouse money. I was pushing a squeaky cart through Food Lion in my FitFlops, which incidentally smelled of old lake slime and fish scales.

But Ned Leavan. His death sent a crackly lightning bolt through my noggin. Here's a guy who looked like me, lived like me. *Was* me. And then there he was feeding the grass at St. John's Cemetery. We'd see each other at the ballgame or the summer lake concert or the big box stores and shake and nod and laugh about the names, the whole doppelgänger thing. "When have you seen the milkman?" he'd go. He meant our secret father, though we knew this wasn't possible. We hoped. Ned was a comfort, a reminder that we're all just a fleck of dust. And then he *was* dust.

As a result, I decided I needed to truly *do* something in honor of the doppelgänger —something productive. I shaved my hair down to the skull, purchased an old blue t-shirt, which I inscribed with "Enforcer" so as to not directly challenge the authority of the authorities—and I affixed my mountain bike with a flashing light and siren I bought on eBay. I camped out at Cumulus Drive and Stratocumulus Circle (the builders had a thing for clouds) with a jug of ice water, a clicker, a clipboard, a used speed gun (also purchased on eBay) and a bag of PB&Js.

You might find this set-up inconceivable or over-the-top, but consider that our fine neighborhood was of the involved school. Neighborhood pictures, festivals, carol singing, block parties. In an era when supposedly nobody knows their neighbors, we knew them all-too-well, Wifey and I. When I began issuing "tickets"—though I referred to them as "issuances" (which perhaps smacked of something both formal and less threatening)—peeps thought nothing of it. They went along. Some (okay, many) drivers even thanked me for my presence—said it helped "calm the traffic." This in lieu of a sign saying "Traffic Calming," which wouldn't pass muster with the neighborhood council.

Precisely the point—calming.

But then there were those who found, let's just say, less to go along with. The speeders, the honkers, the players of loud abrasive music, the fail-to-signal-properly.

I had a template.

I had an eye narrowed on even the slightest infraction. Broken windows theory and all.

So, there I was, standing in the shade, barely visible, under the sweetgum. Waiting.

THE FIRST THREE DAYS, not much happened. No issuances (which was for the best, since the form was a work-in-progress), only some "slow down" gesturing on my part. Most smiled and waved, waved and smiled. I got the finger from two teenagers, one of whom you'll get to know soon. Otherwise, I wondered if my efforts were productive at all.

Wifey wondered the same.

Eating sweet potatoes and sausage (I did the cooking) out on the deck, leafy shadows wriggling about overhead. Wifey looked beaten-down and haggard from her day of labor.

"Please remind me what you are trying to prove exactly," she said, tilting her head. The slightest of shit-eating grins—I knew that one.

"Nothing really. Just something to do to pass the time."

I don't get into doppelgänger politics with Wifey—I know better.

"Why don't you try another head-hunter? Something more directly useful. Something else that, you know, *pays*."

I didn't want to get into that song and dance, either.

"I'm using the search engines...."

"But they have *other* methods."

"I know, but if the first one didn't work...."

"Try *another* one."

"I need to be patient."

I knew she wanted me to return to a gainful state of employment as much for her sanity as mine. Plus, our savings account was hemorrhaging like a third-rate actor in some Tarantino sword fight.

"This is just to occupy myself," I said.

"So, it's masturbation then."

I ate my sausage. Sprinkled more salt and pepper on the sweet potato. It felt good to squish the potato meat with my fork.

ON THE FOURTH DAY, I was actually needed. I arrived at seven-thirty a.m.—I scooted out of the house before the wife was awake. At seven-forty-seven (approximately) a red Buick Skylark clipped through the Stratocumulus stop sign and angled a sharp left directly toward me. I stepped out into the intersection immediately, my hand stretched out like Earl Campbell throwing a stiff arm. The Skylark slammed its brakes to avoid making me a permanent part of the pavement. The guy rolled down the window, threw up his hands and slammed them back down on the steering wheel.

"What the hell are you doing?" Spittle jetted from his mouth.

"Please don't use profanity in the presence of a peacekeeping force," I said. I wanted to use "officer," but chose not to self-incriminate.

"Since when is 'hell' profanity? What is this, 1951? If you want me to use profanity, believe me, I can. And why are you standing in the middle of the freaking road? That's my beef."

But at that point I was already scribbling, checking boxes, and jotting down license plate information. Just like they do. Just like a *real* police officer. And to my surprise he offered up his registration.

Billy Forester, age twenty-one. Five ten, curly hair, bad skin. Sticker from the community college on his rear windshield. Smoking a cigarette.

"This is an issuance—it's a warning. Next time it goes directly to the county police. You need to make sure you come to a full stop at any and all neighborhood stop signs. Children live here. And please refrain from cursing—it's unseemly."

"It's what? An *issuance*? So, it's not even a real ticket?" "So." He liked "so."

"I report to the county police," I said. A slight exaggeration, but not *that* far-fetched.

"So, you're a rent-a-cop or something? Security staff hired by the home owner's association?"

I ignored this comment. "Have a nice day."

"Whatever, man. I'm heading to a job interview." He didn't move. Perhaps it wasn't exactly of the highest order. Perhaps he was not really in a hurry.

"Well, good luck," I said.

"It can't be worse than the Pizza Shack. Those people treat you like *slaves*."

"*If* you get the position," I said.

"Thanks for the boost of confidence." But he said this with such low affect that I wasn't sure if it was sarcastic or straight. He nosed his jalopy off down the road. Not a bad kid, I thought. Just needed to learn a few things. He'd do better next time.

I was pleased by my trial run. Too pleased, I'm sure.

Squatted in the grass in the shade with my radar and my eye on the stop sign. Do enforcers have an innate personality? Is there a natural enforcer psychology that I just happened into by dumb luck? I

never thought of myself as an enforcer, but at that point I was one—
or at least I was actively trying to be. Do enforcers find inherent
value in a bylaw? Does this excite them? I had always believed there
is no inherent value; perhaps I was wrong about that. Perhaps, I
thought, enforcing the law is just another way of finding meaning in
meaninglessness. If I hand out an issuance does this establish a
façade—logic to illogic? Perhaps.

Do what you're thinking. Be in the moment. Fill in the cliché. I
was there for old Ned, I told myself.

This *does* give me meaning, I thought. I'm here doing good,
helping society, one small agent of positivity in a world steeped in
the opposite.

And just as I thought this, I glimpsed a red Chevy Suburban bar-
reling down Cumulus at thirty-eight (speed limit is twenty). I threw
up my hands, stepped out into the street—just like before. Sweat
slavered down my back. "Enforcer" now scrawled on my shirt, my
speed gun in both hands. I yanked the clipboard out from behind my
shorts and clicked my ballpoint, the point of it glinting in the sunshine. I was in heaven.

I COULD'VE stayed there all day and all night, frankly, but my body
eventually craved sustenance and I was charged with providing it.

At five-thirty I packed it in, biked the half a mile back home.

Stood at the stove for forty minutes making a light pasta—a little
shrimp and veggies. If I had my druthers I'd eat standing up, over
the sink. Or pop a giant nutrient pill like they did on the *Jetsons*.

Wifey came home and we ate in front of the game—lest conversation ruin a good thing. Didn't have to think with the sound blaring.
She complimented my cooking during an AT&T commercial. I
smiled and chewed, and it was pleasant. Atmosphere management
works with forty-somethings as well as toddlers.

After dinner we flipped through magazines and I half-watched the game. It was, as often is the case, as if we lived in a waiting room. We were biding time, waiting for something exciting to happen to or in our lives. Other than my layoff, nothing did. And even the layoff was no big deal in the larger scheme of things. We were still eating. We could pay the bills.

Driving around town, I sometimes imagined that something tragic would happen to us—anything to break up the ruthless monotony. My fantasy extravaganza usually landed on house fire—a blazing cauldron, everything up in smoke. She'd blame me; I'd blame her—we'd have a reason to go our separate ways.

Boredom is not inconsequential.

Vacations are the worst: relationship-building, long slow passages of time, extensive magazine flipping. Boredom layered on boredom—an ennui layer cake.

SALLY CARRUTHERS became a frequent nemesis all-too-soon (internally, I referred to her as Sally Struthers). Mauve mini-van, little stick figure decal family on the rear window, perky blonde dye do. And Sally drove like a race car driver.

The first time, she drove so fast I couldn't stop her—she was *by* me before I could even step *to* the curb much less off it. She must've been doing forty-five, fifty. The next time I saw her, I threw up my hands early when she was still a hundred yards out. I then lunged dramatically out into the street. She slammed on her brakes, popped her window open.

"What do *you* want?" She toyed with her hair seductively, beneath the coating of nervousness. Her hands gesticulated as if she had imbibed one too many mocha lattes.

"I think you know. You were speeding, ma'am."

"And who are *you*? I have a meeting. I mean I really have to *move*." The edge of flirtation ceased entirely.

"I'm the enforcer. I'm a *representative* of the law."

She rolled her eyes. "You don't represent squat. Just a *guy*."

I wrote quickly and didn't look up, as to expedite the proceedings before she ran over my feet.

"And why are you in such a hurry?" I flicked my eyes into the foreground for a half a second. Her car looked as though somebody lived in it, which in a sense they did.

"That's none of your business."

I handed her the issuance.

"Gotta be kidding me. This looks like it was made by a third grader."

I shrugged. She had a point there.

"Please slow down before you hurt someone. You're going twice the speed limit. This level of speeding may land you in prison. Is that what you want?"

She shrugged back. Her tires did a little mini-squeal as she took off.

I DON'T for the life of me understand why people simply cannot follow the law. That's why it's called "the law." It rules, not you. When you are dead like Ned, the law will continue. What's right is, after all, what's right. You can question it all you want, but you have to ultimately *live* with it, embrace it. The law has been decided for you; your job is to follow it.

In the text of my issuance, I had a rational application of the real law, a warning system which, if adhered to, would result in greater compliance. I attempted to convey this to the district station, but their responses were thin and far between. I understood—they had other, more important fish to fry. Sizzle, sizzle. *They* were professional enforcers out doing their enforcing thing and I was just a peon. But.

When I'm on the road, I think, I *abide*. I'm one of the only few who *does*. Everyone around me is going fifteen miles an hour faster, no signaling, abusing their horns, their headlights. Ignoring yields.

If I could I would've handed each one of them an issuance. I even went so far as to visualize a scenario whereby I could text an issuance to each offender—someday, I'll zap those jerks.

Nobody respects the law.

I know why this is: we think we can do without it. That is until we need it—until that moment when we are victimized and want justice. Then we embrace the law, except for the looters and the roustabouts who continue to abuse it to their own advantage.

Speeding is no different to me than rape or murder. If a law is broken, a law is broken.

That night an e-mail from dispatch: "please stop sending your reports. We are overwhelmed." "Overwhelmed" will not stop me.

THEN THERE WAS Eduard Gomez and William Wallace—or maybe it was Wallace William (I forget): These guys didn't speed; they stopped and yielded—but they drove so far under the speed limit, their vehicles were all-but-stopped. Backing up traffic. Causing a nuisance. They were the twin sloths of the neighborhood and any time I saw either one of them galumphing down Cumulus I sighed. It was as if they were leading a funeral procession of their own making. And it meant a gravy train of pissed drivers *behind* them— kneading steering wheels, flashing lights, complaining, yelling "what is this shit?"

Each received an issuance, politely, slowly, and without particular remorse.

It wasn't until later I realized they were doppelgängers themselves, of a sort—and that they might not even know of each other's existence.

"DO YOU CONSIDER yourself a hero or something?"

This was Fran, the retired second grade teacher. She was lucky to be five feet, squat and wrinkled. She walked with a limp and wore mirrored sunglasses so dark and reflective I could see myself in her eyes from yards away.

"No, just helping out," I said.

"Are you?"

"Am I what?" It was hot and I dripped with thick sweat, even in the shade.

"Are you really helping out? Do I have to do all the work around here?"

I told her about Ned and his tragic fate. I told her about unemployment checks and the relentless grimace on Wifey's mug. I told her about the need to Enforce, the whole Enforcer ethos.

Hands on arthritic hips, she listened—or pretended to. No nodding or verbal cues, just eyeball-to-eyeball—*Gunsmoke* listening.

"All that is well and good," she said. "But you're *not* the police."

I had heard this before.

"That is true," I said. "I am the man before you get to them. I'm the Enforcer. That's, I think, what—"

"Your warnings—they don't have any teeth, see what I mean? What's the point?"

I didn't have an answer for that. I stood and stared gape-mouthed at the stop sign, at the curb.

"Just helping out," I said.

"I'm Mrs. Straight," she said. She pointed to her face with two crooked fingers. "I live over there. And my *eye* is on you." As if she only had one.

AND SO it went. All day I was "out at the corner," as Wifey said. It was true, not dismissive. I wasn't a pimp. I wasn't selling little baggies of oregano or crushed aspirin. I was attempting to instill order, to straighten out society.

"And what about the job situation? I mean, I don't mind—it's just…"

I ignored questions of this sort.

I know she wanted to say: "We're losing money every month. You realize that, don't you? Savings only goes so far. And then what?"

But she didn't. She offered up a modicum of restraint. I loved her at that moment.

The back of my mind processed the rest. I wanted to curse, but didn't.

"Honey biscuit," I said.

"What?"

"Never mind."

Out on the Cloud intersection I had my usual array of debutantes, pumpkin heads and flakes. And it was searing and sticky, which had me chasing the shade.

Then, at four in the afternoon, just before I was going to call it quits, suddenly there was Fran standing at attention with her toady disposition and eagle eyes.

"I have put a call in," she said. She stood in the pool of sun, just at the lip of the shoulder, as if that would intimidate me.

"Uh-huh," I said, wiping my brow. My water was warm; I itched from the weeds and gnats and dandelion spores.

"The police dontcha know. They are very curious as to what it is you are doing here making claims about being a policeman."

"One—I never claimed to be an official policeman. And two, we're in regular contact," I said. "It's a matter of fact."

"The officer I spoke to had never heard of you *or* your project."

"Well, they're busy, aren't they? I'm sure it is a lot for them to keep track of. You know how it goes."

She limped from the sun, closer to me, into a small oval of shade pooled below the birch tree.

"Let me be frank," she said. "I don't think you are in full possession of your marbles. Sitting out here all day bossing people around—that is not *your* job. And nobody asked for it. Nobody *wants* your help. Who asked for this?"

I waved her off. I wanted to tell her that I'm addressing an obvious need—hasn't she seen the way people drive these days? Hasn't she opened her eyes? But you can't teach an imbecile the history of Russia.

"And furthermore," she continued. The vein in her neck popped and her face looked mottled and bloodshot. "You strike me as someone who suffers from a complex. You're trying to overcome something here by telling *my* neighbors what to do. Take up a hobby or something, will you? It's not our fault."

What I wanted to say but didn't was that *they* were my neighbors too—that's the whole point. I wanted to tell Fran about my dead doppelgänger and duty and how I may be floundering but the whole complex thing is a projection, an invention. Plus, she's not exactly a bastion of society, I wanted to say. Clearly.

But I said nothing. I decided the high road was best for all concerned—otherwise I'd have to throw her into the lake.

"Thank you for your feedback," I said, waving to her.

This was the beginning of the end though: I could tell. She had a thread and I was the sweater.

TWO DAYS LATER, Officer Statton was introducing himself and issuing me a ticket (a real ticket) for impersonating a police officer. Tall man with shoulders as wide as the doorway, hair skull-tight.

"But how am I impersonating you? I wasn't wearing a uniform. The forms are different. My shirt clearly says 'Enforcer," not 'Police.'" I had zero motivation to argue, but I was hoping to find some way to continue the progress I had made.

His face was a bland, uninterested prairie. "That's what *we* are, sir," the officer said. "*We* enforce."

So, I was compelled to remove myself from the corner and the neighborhood in general in terms of staking my claim to any sort of ticketing or traffic stoppages. I could only return to my corner sans gear, as a "normal civilian."

Such is life, I knew even then.

I'm not about to offer some grand denouement which spins everything already mentioned into some kind of meaningful, tidy little bundle so you can feel better about yourself and your own pathetic insights and judgments. I'm not going to lie to you.

My wife left me a few months after my enforcing stint ended and I was forced to sell the house. Luckily, I got just under one hundred K from the proceeds, which was more than enough to pay the rent on a shabby little one bedroom for a while (I sleep on a decade-old blow-up mattress on the floor). It bought beer, also. My wife won't talk to me; she says I'm bad Juju. She wishes I would just roll over and croak.

As for a job, I hear the Pizza Shack is hiring dishwashers, and I may even apply. There are worse things. I always was good with my hands and it might be healing in some way (though the thought of wet, gnawed-upon food bits floating in the water near my arms makes me quasi-nauseous).

Sometimes I head back into the old neighborhood and sit at my old corner. I bring a counter and just count the cars go by with a single click of my thumb. No issuances, no pretenses of anything other than watching. Nobody notices me and now that it's November and chilly and dark. I stand to keep the blood flowing. The grass is stiff with frost during the mornings. It will be winter soon, and then spring again. Next year can only be better, can't it?

IT CAN'T HURT, CAN IT?

☛

WHEN I SAY "testify" I don't mean this in any traditional slash Christian sense. No baptisms, or the like. Nor do I mean "testify" in the legal sense. I simply and directly am implying a simple and direct statement testifying as to the truth-quality of my position. I don't mean to sound pretentious; I am known to be anything but.

The first thing you should be aware of is that I practice a cutting-edge slash alternative form of Reiki which I like to call "remote Reiki." The United Federation of Touchless Touch Masters has determined that I am the second most highly ranked Reiki practitioner in the region—not that I keep an active tally or the like (these are, of course, subject to trends and fancy, and this also frequently shifts according to the high-drama of Reiki-whimsy; it's all political). There is an ebb and flow to such things.

This story starts and ends with remote Reiki.

It also starts and ends with Ed. Ed is my husband.

You may consider it odd for someone named Charlotte Felicity Emily Grainsborough (that's me, CFEG) to find herself betrothed to a gentleman who goes by the name of Ed, however, I would remind you that his full nomenclature is Edward Williams Williamson. He prefers "Ed."

What happened over the long course of our marriage is this: though we commenced in synch in virtually every way—spiritually,

emotionally, psychologically, philosophically, mentally, gastronom-
ically, astrologically—the air slowly hissed out of the balloon of our
marriage to such a degree that nine months later I wasn't so sure
anymore. Edward was identifiably exact to the man who proposed
to me, tears galloping down his face as he mouthed Whitney Houston
to me under a delicate gossamer array of pink and purple and white
floral arrangements. Yes, perhaps his overindulgence in margaritas
assisted such pathos; however, who's to say this wasn't also the
emergence of his identifiably authentic self? Perhaps his true self
was dormant, ready to erupt from the normalcy of daily living.

But, as my mentor likes to say, "One year is a long spell to unite
with any one soul."

I miss Ed: he is still my best friend and soul mate.

That said, I additionally believe we all possess more than one
soul mate. Perhaps an entire yellow school bus chock-filled with
soul mates awaits each of us. And on that bus of soul mates, each
soul mate frolics with the other soul mates, on occasion, in wait for
potential union with the soul mate who is us. Who wouldn't want a
ride on *that* bus?

THERE WAS NOT one specific moment that brought the house of mar-
ital cards tumbling down. There were many.

Ed claims, however, that the incident with Jarvis was the straw
that broke his lovelorn back.

To clarify: Jarvis was (and is) a client of the first order. He is
what we within the Reiki community call a "steadfast"—a weekly
customer who sought not only a "quick fix" for his ailments, as most
do, but truly a continual lifestyle alteration and improvement. Needless to say, Jarvis was (and is) a highly valued Reiki nook.

Which is why I saw little problem (much less a conflict of interest) with Jarvis reclining au natural, privates a-jutting as I wandered
my hands invisibly—close but not touching—over his protuber-

ances. He complained of testicular numbness and overall genital disturbances unmoved by the appearance of womanly beauty. I revealed this simply and directly to Edward, but he remained stubbornly convinced that something extra-ordinary slash interpersonal slash quasi-erotic may have been afoot between yours truly and Mr. Jarvis.

Anything could be farther from the truth.

In actuality, it was the interruption Edward provided which caused the said Jarvis protrusion to wane and caused the overall healing process to retard significantly. In other words, though my husband views Jarvis's nakedness as a sign of his cuckoldry, as Philip P. Seaman Esq. has informed me, a suit against Edward in pursuance of lost wages is not entirely out of the question.

To wit: point seven of such a line of reasoning—my designated home office space was at the time affixed with a "Please Knock" sign, which was conveniently ignored by my husband at the moment of my so-called "indiscretion." A "Please Knock" sign is not only a request (says Philip P. Seaman Esq.), but an invisible contract between members of such residence. Willfully ignoring such a sign is a breach of unwritten contract by one such member of such residence, and such a breach in itself is worthy of damages paid in full.

Who said that hovering a healing hand above another man's erect penis and taut scrotal skin constitutes infidelity? Was there touching? Did seed emerge from such a healing state? Does the Bible make mention of legitimate and documented Reiki techniques upon a wounded groin? This was a healing act related 110% to my professional acts and it was entirely within the bounds of UFTTM guidelines and procedures.

SPEAKING OF REIKI, I now realize the crux of the problem is this: I was stubbornly practicing Reiki in person rather than taking advantage of a much larger and infinitely more lucrative *remote* Reiki market. In this light, the betrayal by Edward was a helpful pointer: I grasped then and there that I must sever the chains which tie me to in-person healing and instead embrace a much larger community— the world itself! I could constantly hover! I could be a healing cloud in the cloud!

As Edward stewed and worse (more on this in a moment) as a result of "the Jarvis incident," as I began calling it, I simply decided to be proactive, to take the high road (tolls need not apply).

This high road, unfortunately, involved posting ads online and sending hundreds of millions of e-mails to various addresses I had acquired over the years. I became, I suppose, a kind of Reiki spammer in my attempt to salvage my connubial relations.

By this point, Ed had hunkered down at the Red Roof Inn off 216, watching horse racing and drinking beer and kicking his sadsack heart around the shabby beige industrial carpet. I still felt empathy.

"Why don't you let me try it?" His voice was thin, almost weakened. However, it could've been the Red Roof echo-chamber.

"I just need to take a few antacids, Charl." He was in denial; the phone plastic felt cool against my neck. I could feel the emergence of a strong vein of positivity.

"You know, it can't hurt," I said.

"Yes, it can."

"How?"

"It can hurt my soul," he said. "Deeply. My confidence. Everything."

"I'm going to anyway," I said. I began my complex set of preparations.

"You can't forcibly Reiki me," he said.

"But I can *heal* you remotely," I said. "And you won't even know it. You're still my husband, Edward."

"Only going by Ed now. I've told you this."

"Reiki isn't a verb, by the way. It's 'heal.' Healing is the action."
This was our repartee; this was where our relationship landed.

A few more exchanges and Edward disengaged. He muttered a sentence about needing to quash my maternal instinct, or something to this effect, in his parlance.

I continued my preparations and performed my healing anyway: who says one can't compel a horse to drink from water?

By the next day his intestinal complaints had diminished (I failed to ask him about antacids then). He still said he was forcibly Reikied. It's a kind of spiritual rape, he said. But I had already chosen to ignore him.

POST-HEALING, I must almost always, in addition, cleanse myself. I must expunge the accumulated filth from my qi. My healing process has to do with seeking my own center, and then crawling into my own center so that my center takes the shape of a kind of nest of energy which encapsulates me in such a way that it takes on its *own* energy. It is only when the energy of my center-nest exceeds my own energy that I know I can return to the activities of mankind.

These activities often revolve around gustatory matters (one of the ironies of my husband's post-flight maladies). I told him that if he ingests the shell of a robin's egg along with sufficient dandelion seeds this would perfectly compliment my healing gestures on his behalf. Little did he listen! My balance has to do with not just rudimentary matters as minerals and vitamins, but more or less with the *tone* of what I ingest. For instance, I usually find that positivity arrives with the consumption of orange foods on even-numbered days. To wit, on the 18th of an even numbered month, I find myself dining on clementine wedges and tangerines, carrots and saffron-spiced rice. On oddly numbered days it's blue or green, or some combination of the two—broccoli and cabbage and blueberries and avocados.

ED WAS at the door three days after our healing session (whether or not he was aware of such session). Thankfully for his displaced sense of bourgeois morality, I was not involved with healing male genitalia at this juncture. Also, the current state of the economy has put a dent in the Reiki market (remote or otherwise).

Ed clutched a handful of garbage bags.

"Came to get some stuff, Charl," he said. He was not unshaven, which was a pleasant surprise. However, I could tell he had returned to the habit of meat ingestion—his body reeked of animal fat (I maintain a fine-tuned sense of smell).

"Sure," I said.

"I don't want a scene," he said.

It sounded like some cliché from a hack 90's-era film starring Sandra Bullock. It was disappointing.

"No," I simply said.

He stepped inside.

"What the hell?"

He was referring to the fact that by this point in the downward slope of our relationship, I had painters glaze the entirety of my 3,623.25 square feet abode in turquoise. My mentor said cool, fish-bowl-esque colors would soothe me.

"I feel like some kind of sea cucumber, Charl."

"Well, good. That's the general idea. Or part of it. Why don't you come back? This is soothing, you have to admit."

He blew his nose into his sleeve; he knows how I find this to be counter-productive to his much-depleted energies.

"It's a bit too...weird here for me," he said. "I just came to get some clothes. And I'm tired of wearing the same shirt. I am not even a Pittsburgh Pirates fan."

"Be my guest," I said. "Can I make you a bean sprout and edamame wrap? It's the twenty-fifth."

"See," he said, walking away. "That's exactly what I mean. I don't believe in that, in any of that."

I told him there was nothing to believe; uber-organic, numerological gustatory practices have been proven worldwide to promote energy construction. To wit, the article in *Sea Kelp Monthly*.

I STILL, sadly, associate the Tuvan throat music with Edward's final steps away from the love that once was ours. Long marriages, I assume, must find conclusion in one way or another. My mentor was the one who convinced me of this. I told her that eleven point two four months is not a particularly long stretch, but my mentor made the excellent point that this is only in *Earth* time. In the inner landscape where we all actually reside, our love lasted for eons. I mentioned to her the insight that Edward and I only had the rare occasion to share the intimacy that is the exchange of holy matrimonial fluids, but my wise mentor said this is no matter.

"The thrust of your love," she said, "is *eternal*, not merely physical. Keep the flame alive in your soul."

At any rate. I have chosen respite in the form of pillows. My mentor said pillows would help defuse the emotional violence of Ed's departure. I journeyed to one of our local home and bath retailers and pursued this line of thinking to the tune of twenty-nine pillows. All aquamarine. Now I live within a *soft* fish tank, Ed says.

The use of the present tense is purposeful. I am still in active touch with my husband. I still conduct healing upon him in the form of remote Reiki, whether he shares this knowledge or not. He did mention to me not to "talk about that shit no more." At least he does refrain from clearing his nasal passages into his clothing in my presence.

I have subsequently found a wondrous new soul mate from the bus of soul mates which is our spherical orb. She emerged from the doors of the bus with an energy that bespoke of her royalty and divine spirit. Her name is Thistle Bud Chillington. Our union is *purely* nonsexual, and will remain so—as I physically lean towards the pull of the protuberances of men—but she has embraced Reiki remote and otherwise with open wings. She adores the cool rapture of my azure walls and the pillows which I have towered hither and thither to suit my own healing purposes.

We drink tea together with vast abandon. My heart swells in the whirlpools of chai.

As it turns out, I am now her mentor and am in the process of instructing her in the process and methodology of Reiki remote and otherwise. The future is a vast plain on the bottom of the endless sea that is my voyage. And on this sea my healing is ceaseless.

HUGGERS NOT MUGGERS!

☛

EVERYONE HATES The Huggers. Even The Huggers must hate The Huggers, because how could they not? Their lives consist of tooling around from one regional store to another doling out "necessary tips." It's a meeting. It's a PowerPoint. It's a step-by-step. It's a pop-up motivational session. They do post-chat video monitoring, all that jazz. We are to follow their dictums to the letter, Stone says. "Ask no questions—it will be less painful if you just bend over and take it."

So, I wake up in a sour piss mood, as my sister Carmen used to call it. Low on coffee, drinking weak tea. Low on food. Ironic since I work at a grocery store. I eat a breakfast biscuit, a chalky hard-boiled egg and brace myself for the blast of evil air outside. They're calling for a heavier slurry of wintery mix tonight. "Wintery mix"—sounds almost festive, something you might hear at a club. Give it up for the "wintery mix, ya'll! Brrrrrrrrrrrrrrrrrrrrrrrrrrrrrrrrrrrrrrrrrrrrrr." To me all it means is more work, a pile on. Scraping windshields, shoveling, tending to the pipes, salt, cat litter, digging in pockets for hat and gloves.

Which is what I'm doing out there in the damp dawn, sun buried below the horizon and under the weight of heavy steely cloud cover. Haven't seen the sun in ten days.

When Huge found itself bought out by the Norwegians five years ago I knew I should've left. Pre-Norwegians, Huge was low-key,

well-organized, union-driven and flexible. All that. I'm probably
overly romanticizing, naturally—but not by much. Post-Norwegians,
it's higher end, all about flashy goods, less about prices for the buyer.
The Norwegians proclaimed "Americans will spend more money for
a higher quality product. Americans like high-end." Grocery spending is up eighteen percent over the last two years alone. Luxuries up
the wazoo. That takes into account inflation, also.

My drive to Huge sucks the life out of me, but it's also when I
get most of my writing done—that's how slow the traffic is. I have
a little notebook and a dinky little pen and I scribble frantic miniature
words in between glances up at the vehicular molasses creep. Recently I've been daydreaming about quitting writing altogether—
just retiring, another unpublished writer bites the dust. Well, I've
self-published one poorly written, poorly edited book—*Gravy
Train*—about three canned-gravy salesmen in the 60's, at the cusp
of the mass-produced, mass-marketed bullshit in which we currently
swim. I can't bear to look at it, lest I notice yet another glaring typo
that I ignored or missed in the hurry to find a handful of readers un-
related to me. But the plot is preposterous and the tone is all wrong
and the characters are over-the-top and somehow strike me as based
on The Lion, Scarecrow and Tin Man, though all of this happened
at a subconscious level and it's the worst kind of second-guessing.
And I didn't really do my homework on gravy, so despite my best
intentions, the book rings untrue. It's terrible. I sold five copies, four
to my mother and one to some guy in Arkansas who probably really
likes gravy and buys everything on the subject (Gravy fetishist?). I
got the idea at Huge, of course. And now, as a result, I view with
suspicion any idea that comes to me when I'm working.

Of course, quitting writing would take place, in my fantasy, long
after quitting Huge. Huge wouldn't even merit a thought, except I
have to live it. Huge is me and I am Huge. This makes for a difficult
separation.

It's so cold my windshield is a smear of half-frozen windshield wiper liquid and bird shit and salt and grime.

"HOWDY," I say. My normal entry.

Lyn Fields is the first to greet me. This is not unusual. I put my yellow and orange uni on, affixed with the button that reads, "Huge loves Hugs, too!" with an over-the-top winking emoticon after the exclamation mark.

"A blessed day to you," she says.

Lyn is mousy and so pale I can see her capillaries. This morning she's wearing one of those Pippi Longstockingesque hats (blue, green and red) and glancing over her pocket Bible at the chipped break table. She has that "touched glow" all over her cheeks and eyes, filled with beneficence and angelic vibrations, like some kind of born-again Christian doll version of herself. Yet, I can see that she isn't one for self-maintenance. Her glasses are rimmed with a greenish, mossy discoloration (would someone please lend her some eyeglasses cleaner shit once a year?). If only somebody loved her, but it would be a salvage job...Single as far as I know.

"Hey."

"Oh, did you get the text?"

No, I didn't because my ex-girlfriend took my cell phone and my other gadgets when we broke up three weeks ago. That's what I get for involving myself with a kleptomaniac (I knew that going in). I don't explain; I just shake my head. Nobody loves anybody, I think.

"Meeting is happening at seven thirty. Not noon."

"Seven-thirty?" That's just great. "Great."

"Seven-thirty. Sven says it's much more of a down time in terms of traffic and such. He's right about that."

"Everyone's gotta be right sometimes."

Lyn bows. If Lyn had a backbone and stuck up for us to Sven even once or twice, our lives would be far easier. But she's just the

assistant manager. Grant Stone, who is off on administrative leave
for diverting from the music station requirement one afternoon, is
not much more helpful. His streaks of rebellion only bubble up in
small, insignificant ways. Lyn is filling in.

Jorge salutes us and then Billy ambles in, smoothing his ponytail
and Vickie exhales audibly at the display. Harry does his morning
lunges near the refrigerator, performing them in quick stabbing
bursts. Mary, Lyn tells us, will be on Express but she's the only one
who gets to skip out on The Huggers. The rest of us have to suck it
up. Until their arrival, we stock and dawdle and grumble and hide
in the dark corners. Pretty soon, there will be far too much light.

Jorge lifts his head from his phone.

"Calling for more snow," he says.

"Yeah," I say.

I pull out my Free Hug coupon. Good for a minimum of one hug
from any team member. I hand it to Jorge and he opens his arms
wide. Then I wave him off.

"Are you sure?"

"Quite," I say.

We smile. We've been through this routine before. He knows I
loathe hugs. If I acknowledge the shit in my future, I will handle it
better, I know.

I NEEDED that to get me through. Ten minutes later it's Sven and Gloria, his wife-to-be. We're crouched on the break room floor and Sven
holds his smart phone out like a flashlight and beams images on the
wall.

"Greetings, Huge team members! Doesn't it feel wonderful to
hear that? 'Team members.' 'Huge!' It means you are part of a team.
And do you know what a team also is? A family. We are a Huge family. Hahahahaha, that sounds like a good thing to be a part of, doesn't
it? Just think of me as Uncle Sven. Hahahahahaha."

Sven is seven feet tall and blonde and rail thin. His fingers must be a foot long, I swear. He's like some further evolved human from the future come to prod us for his entertainment. And he's not Norwegian. He used to work at our store, in fact, before he got "bumped up" to the motivational team. Then he changed his name to something more "appropriate," he said. Something exotic. Something unreachable. Ladder climber. We don't know how this works. Meaning me.

Sven speaks with a blander version of a Wisconsin accent.

We nod and mumble. He's really just a guy and we envy the hell out of him.

"I'm sorry, what was that?" He's smiling, ear to shining ear.

"Yes, Sven."

Gloria nods in agreement.

The first PowerPoint slide shows a smiling (of course) cartoon Huge team member wearing his yellow uni greeting a smiling (of course) female customer. Their PowerPoints utilize cartoons, never ever real people.

"Hello!" It reads.

"A good hello is actually quite difficult to achieve," Sven says. "Let's hear you all say 'Hello'!"

"Hello," most of us dully intone.

"Let's try that again, this time with Huge Family feeling!"

"Hello!" we mumble somewhat more emphatically.

"When we greet the customers, it is imperative that we offer a hearty Hello! Not a muttered, disaffected hello. An honest, hearty hello. Sometimes we must find the inner hello deep inside of us. There are times we must tease out the earnest greeting."

The next frame shows the male cartoon Huge team member with a half-hearted smile, looking off in the other direction. The female cartoon customer looks perplexed and her brows are furrowed. Her arms look far too long—out of proportion to her body.

"Nobody likes to be discounted, to feel like a slime mold on the bottom of some forgotten, clammy sea. We all want appreciation and a care or three."

I hate it when Sven gets faux-folksy—he is nothing close to folksy and never will be and his façade comes across as contrived and sarcastic, though he means for it to sound earnest. Even worse.

"Let's practice our hearty hello one more time."

"Helloooooooooo! Helloooooooooooo!"

"Perfect, nicely done. Effective timbre."

Next slide. "So, what is the right way to utter a hello? How does a team member go about this artful exchange effectively?" The slide is of a cartoon cashier surrounded by pink and green and purple question marks.

Step 1: look the customer in the eyes. The customer, unlike some dogs, will not see this as a threat—the eye contact.

Pic of a smiling vintage cartoon dog. Mild-mannered laughter.

Step 2: "Smile. Always a good rule of thumb, of course."

Pic of a smiling young oddball.

Step 3: "Utter 'hello" or 'hello' plus one greeting or more. With the smile still in place as much as possible. No more than hello plus one. Otherwise it does confuse the customer, and studies have shown that a confused customer has a twenty-seven percent chance of fleeing the store entirely, and there's a ninety percent chance he or she will never shop at the offending store again.

This is not as easy as it sounds.

Next slide: smiling cartoon cashier and smiling cartoon customer.

Everyone is now happy, like old friends who just happen to be in the midst of winning the lottery in a grocery store.

Sven and his yes-woman prattle on for twenty minutes more on the art of hello but it fails to make a dent in our collective cynicism.

"Thank you, Huge family. We kindly appreciate your efforts and hope we can honor you in the same way you honor us. Sven stands rod-straight, his freakishly large head nearly brushing the break room paneled ceiling. His alien fingers click his smart phone. "Now go out there and greet some customers. There are enough of them to go around."

We trudge off to where we must be.

I AM lucky. At one-fourteen I get a fifteen-minute break. At this time Lyn happens to be heating up a frozen bean burrito. The burrito smells like scorched Styrofoam. Which is scorched oil. Which must be cancer causing. Which=death.

"Hey," she says.

"Hey," I say, trying not to gag at the stench of her cancer death burrito.

"The Huggers are something," she says. "I sure hope they find a way to peer past the limitations of this world. They have ideals."

She sounds a bit crazier every time she speaks.

"Yeah, well—they are in charge.

"This is a problem then," she says.

This is nothing new. She is just more aware than usual.

"Yes, I suppose that is true," I say. "But what can we do?"

Lyn tells me our store is going bonkers over pay cuts and increased meetings. With The Huggers. "Efficiency," they call it. As in, by having an increased load of meetings we are more "efficient" than before. It would be easy to make the converse case.

"What if I apply to be a Hugger myself? What would you say to this?"

"Bless you, my child," she says. She reminds me immediately of some nineteenth-century school mom. She has that affect upon me. "I doubt they would cater to that though, Hugh."

"You never know!" My bogus sprightliness makes me vomit inside my heart. Also, I have no idea why I care, other than a low-percentage ploy to stick it to Sven, dig up some dirt—kiddie porn, tax evasion, something. Everything they stand for is just too impossibly polished and glistening for me.

"No, you do know. But waste your time with this if you like. You know, The Huggers are plucked from above."

"From God?"

"Don't be so smart."

Her burrito is done and steaming up her mossy glasses. Perhaps the burrito steam causes the algae blooms in the first place. She does like those things.

I TEXT Sven.

Five days later I receive a response: "Srry 4 the delay! Hugging it up! Sure, let's chat. Tomorrow at six A.M. sharp?"

Jiminy Cricket, don't these people ever do things at a "normal" time?

I arrive at the Gas 'Em Up at five-forty four, snag a cup of thin coffee and sit in my frozen car, bleary-eyed.

Beep-beep behind me, Sven waving and smiling inanely. I leave the coffee in my car (big mistake) and he pops the passenger side door open for me. Huge Escalade.

It's like a drug deal, without the drugs.

"Why, hello there, stranger!" Sven says. Is he *perennially* perky? He just saw me the week prior. "What's cooking? How goes it on the so-called front lines? You know, teammates like you are the most valuable component of the Huge empire. You know how valued you are, don't you?"

I shake my head. He's utterly loathsome.

He holds out his clenched fist and I tap it. He must think I'm in first grade. He opens his palm and inside is a sticker with a grinning brontosaurus.

"For you, just a little pick-me-up."

He chuckles.

"Thank you. I put the sticker on, but I can feel the adhesive part is weak."

"I saw your question. You want to become part of 'The Huggers,' as you call us? More like me? I'm just kidding about that last part, of course. You do."

"I'm curious. Change of pace, you know."

"Not really. Not exactly. Why would you want a change of pace?"

"I don't know, you know." Coffee back in my car. Now cold.

"Not exactly regarding the 'you know.' I've always put a premium on consistency and stick-to-it-ness. These are traits you have, I'm certain. But why would you want to leave the front lines? That's where it's at. Huge needs you!"

"Didn't you also—"

"Yes, but it wasn't by choice. Central tapped me. They saw that I might be able to be more….directive. It's different."

"I see."

"So, it's all about doing your best Huge job and maybe then you will become noticed. They are watching. They read the Huge reports. Be Huge and Huge will reward."

"I see. I can't just….apply?"

"Give me your best hug. Right now."

So, I do, slappity-slappy, all whistling fabric and back patting in the sub-zero cold so as to affirm my secure and confirmed heterosexuality.

He nods. Not bad, he says. Not bad.

We will be in touch, if we can use you. Otherwise, please do keep on carrying on. Blah, blah.

"Can you tell me how to improve my hug technique?"

Sly smile. "That's not really my place, now is it, Hugh?"

"My name is one omitted letter away from full gratuitous mirroring."

"I am aware of that. Though one could argue that it is a coincidence."

I ignore that.

"*Is* it a coincidence?"

"What other explanation can you have?"

I smile but don't answer. Let him marinate in mystery for a few seconds.

I'M ZONED OUT in the dairy section, not a good section for zoning out. Right hand out, yogurt in slot. Back to case, right hand out, yogurt in slot. Yogurt. Lyn has me stocking yogurt, which is about the last thing I'd like to deal with. First of all, I hate yogurt—phlegmy glue is all it is to me. Secondly, it's cold (and I'm already plenty cold without yogurt's help). Thirdly, though stocking takes less mental energy, I feel I'm exiled in some grocery store version of Siberia. Sometimes, I'll ditch my outlier position just to get two minutes of social time. I just walk away from several cases of yogurt on the excuse that I need something up front. What, I have no idea. An invoice or something? A price check? Human contact is all.

I see customers swoosh by and I ignore them.

As I'm stocking, I'm simultaneously trying to figure out some way that I can compete with Sven, find some entry point into The Huggers. What did he do to gain access? It's so incredibly shady. The Huggers are just a closed circuit without any real entry point. So you're tapped from someone who is impressed by you, is that it?

Maybe if I enjoyed hugging more, I'd have a better chance. My ex-girlfriend says I'm either all or nothing on the touching thing. I sometimes do feel as though I might get hives from a hug. I'm that type. I have ranted on Craigslist about the ethos of hugging: for instance, on the expectations of hugging even the most remote acquaintance. I'll take a hello and a handshake any day, thank you kindly. Haphebobia or something, perhaps.

The Huggers have infected my brain, like some kind of perky guano bacteria injected right into my squishy cranium.

That night I try to write, but like a ignoramus, I simply stare at the cursor blinking off and on. I'm thinking about The Huggers as some kind of secret club which has shut me out. Just like the secret club of literary agents and decent publishers and readers. I don't know how to gain access to them, either. Even the cursor hates me. It represents a wall of flickering frustration.

TWO DAYS LATER, Lyn calls me in to her little cubbyhole of an office next to the men's room. I'm hoping this is about getting promoted to The Huggers. Then I could look down on the peons as I hugged them, and smirked, and shot smug little PowerPoints out of my ass (I *do* realize this is not the most productive attitude). I could lord my stupid in-crowdness over them all.

"It's a blessed day," she says. "Well, actually, not as blessed as I'd like, actually."

I smell a rat. She hands me a lime green Huge t-shirt emblazoned in pink bubble font "Huggers, Not Muggers!"

"Great, thank you," I say. I'll put it with the rest, in the grocery bag under my bed.

"What's the deal?"

"Sven and Gloria have called to alert me to the fact that you are not greeting the customers when you are on the floor."

I think back and realize they are right.

"Okay," I say, not giving myself up.

"We need to work on *positivity* pronto. Think back to the session from last week. Look them in the eye and smile and say a friendly hello. That's all you need to do."

"Or else what?"

She winces. That wince means it won't be good for me.

Fine. I'm at station six—cashiering, thankfully. Every customer who comes through gets a hug, I decide. Fuck it. I don't like hugs, they are awkward—but we'll smush uglies until someone cries uncle. Let the legal team figure it out. Make the best of a bad situation. "I hate hugs," I tell each one of them—In fact I *detest* them. But here I am hugging you to save my job and to spread general positivity and to underscore corporate culture that tells us we must be intimate on some level so that they can firm up their bottom dollar. Can't miss *that*. I'm supposed to offer customers a feeling of home, a sense that we care, and what better way than a hug? A simple hello is clearly not enough, will not do.

Some customers like the hug, telling me that it is a refreshing reminder of the need for interpersonal connection. Some shrink from me or pat my back quickly, signifying their discomfort. Some ask if this is a store policy (I tell them it is). Some tell me I am actually a very good hugger and that I should embrace my hugging side more fully, despite my phobia. I write out coupons for free hugs, for those interested.

After ten or eleven customers, Lyn strides up behind me, pulls me aside, waves a single finger as if she's scolding me.

"Just the hello will be plenty," she hushes when the line has dwindled. "Maybe, 'how is your day going'?"

Right—leave the hugging to The Huggers.

Next morning, I get the call from Sven. I've stepped across the line. Hugging other team members is fine, but we can't really, you know, risk hugging customers, not yet.

"A hearty hello is all we need from you. I understand the impulse, but actually," he says. "We'll have you on eggs, cheese and yogurt for a while, if you don't mind. It's just easier this way. Plus, you are a *great* yogurt stocker. Best in the store."

"I guess this means I won't be among The Huggers any time soon."

"We don't really use that phrase, 'Huggers,' by the way. Is that something of your own invention?"

"It's been around," I say. I'm aware of the vagueness.

FOR YEARS I've been training myself to dream on-call. It doesn't always work. I sit in the bathroom, listening to the toilet run for twenty minutes, just concentrating on the narrative I want my subconscious to tell itself later. I want to have the Lyn-falls-off-a-cliff dream as I watch, lounging from my leather recliner, sipping an expensive glass of Bordeaux. Really, I would examine Lyn's face—the shocked expression as she realizes the ground is suddenly not there, not anymore, would be, in itself, worth it.

But when I go to sleep, I'm too spun up and my mind churns too close to the surface of things, and the sudden storm that rushes through the area keeps me pinned to rain and wind, maple helicopters pinging against the siding. The dream fails to materialize. In the morning, I have to make do with a quick fantasy that Lyn steps out onto my local neighborhood thoroughfare only to be leveled by a line of motorcycles, one after another after another.

Nothing is going to change—I can see that. I will not be a Hugger, no matter how many hugs I proffer. I will not get a raise. I will not live in a house that I own. My life will be one long Huge drone.

And then I will die.

I'm stuck at the worst traffic light in history. The timing of this particular light is so poor on this thing that it typically takes four rounds to finally make it through. This is my writing place. But today I have my book *The Gravy Train* and I'm calling Lyn on speaker phone.

I get the voicemail.

"Lyn—how are you? I know we were chatting yesterday about self-improvement and ways that my efforts for Huge might go noticed rather than unnoticed, so I thought I would share a little something with you. This is from an unknown masterpiece by the name of *The Gravy Train*. Chapter 7. Jimmy Brown doesn't like townhouses. Why? The thing with townhouses is that they are built around the notion of sameness. They don't even pretend to be different or to aspire to anything other than cookie cutter. There is really nothing wrong with cookie cutter, Jimmy Brown thinks. Except when one gets trapped inside the cookie cutter. You're the dough and on all sides, you are confronted with aluminum. Jimmy knocks on unit number 789, the end unit. He can hear a squall from inside, or perhaps it's from the unit next to that. The walls are so thin."

"My point is this, Lyn—not everything has to be the same for everyone all the time. Exceptions can be made. We can think for ourselves, I think. I think we still can. I do apologize for hogging up your voice mail time. I hope I didn't gum things up—that would be bad. I would never want to gum things up for you. Or The Huggers. Or the Huge Family." Hahahaha.

Of course, I cleaned up the written typos in my oral reading. She'd never know the difference. I have a *real* family—I don't need another bogus one.

I knew I would, one day, eat my dinner from a can of cat food. seventy-eight, seventy-nine maybe. Nobody would touch me and I wouldn't touch them. I would disappear into the ether and receive my hugs from the clouds. I slip my new t-shirt over my head. Of course, it fits perfectly.

HEAD TO TOE

☞

SCALP

We construct ourselves, my father says. We're in the den in the old house. Nobody lives here anymore and he can't sell it. Shame. So he rents it out to whoever is available.

He has built a fire. Outside, the air is damp and cool. A thin fog lurks in the maples.

"Let me put this one in the box," he says. We talk about the mottled and imperfect void.

My father collects thoughts.

He never writes them down.

With his thumb he picks at his scalp until it bleeds. I've told him he should get dandruff shampoo at the very least. He says this is a mere Band-Aid.

"When I sell it," he says. "Then you can retire, then we can do this more often."

By "this" he means speak to me. Collect additional ideas. QT.

EAR LOBES

He refused to let me pierce my ears. I still haven't and can't bear to even look at earrings. He programmed me.

When mother died, I was twelve—at the cusp. It was best that she died. She never smoked, so the lung cancer seemed especially shocking and catastrophic. This is an understatement. Listening to her breathe was an exercise in masochism. She was a drowning fish.

I take my father on walks through the park. The flowers coil and coalesce. They seem to crest over one another, seeking heat and water.

We live in the jungle of the megalopolis.

"You wonder about so many things when you reach my age," he says. "The missing parts, all those gaps."

A witness might comment that it is odd to hear a chicken producer speak in these terms. My father is number three after Perdue and Tysons. He has met his goals. I would like to offer an insight to him, something to add to his collection. But I can't. I'm weary from work.

I will be wealthy one day, but I don't feel like a spoiled trust funder.

And my ears remain holeless, aside from the two canals God has given me.

Chin

My father has a way of lifting his head when he hopes to gain my attention. I notice these things. It's as if he points to me with his chin.

"Have you spoken with him?"

My brother, he means. Zachary. I am in an unfortunate position.

Zachary is in Laos, living on a farm. Growing bamboo. Orchids. Hashish. Scruffy beards. Tofu and Thai basil. My father doesn't speak with Zachary. They haven't seen each other since 2007.

"No," I lie. We usually e-mail about once a week. "You know how he is."

"I do know how he is."

My father stirs his iced tea with a butter knife. The ice cubes clink. He sniffs. I can tell this is a sniff of annoyance, of trying to keep it together emotionally/mentally/psychologically.

"I'd like to see him again."

I don't say the obvious—Zachary is in *Laos*. It's not easy.

"I'll let you know when I hear from him, dad," I say.

It's not going to happen.

CLAVICLE

I am forlorn. I haven't been touched in years, haven't made love in many more years. When I think of my uterus I think of the Mojave in winter.

It's okay—there is more to life than sexual fulfillment. Still, I am forlorn.

I have shown my father a few shots I've taken of myself. Not the full frontal nudes per se—but some of the others. I took one of the webbing of my right foot. I focus closely in on it in such a way that it becomes its own thing—an abstraction.

He appreciated the one of my right clavicle. It looks like a thick sewing needle, or perhaps something from a nautical exhibit on narwhales. My clavicle glows in the light, and the rest is in shadow.

I have sent some of the other images to friends—mostly women friends. This gives me some sense of uplift. I run my finger along my clavicle bone, sometimes without thinking. This alone, for now, is enough.

RIBS

I don't enjoy going there, but he needs my help. Mostly, it gives me nightmares—which stresses me out and exhausts me. But he needs my help and my love for my father supersedes my disgust for the "harvesting," as he calls it.

This takes place in an immense building surrounded on all sides by pine trees. I've asked my father, and he tells me the pine trees are both a sound and (more importantly) smell barrier.

The chickens are killed quickly, as humanely as possible, my father says. It is over in less than five seconds, on average.

Still, there is something unsettling about seeing an animal hang from its feet, then dipped in scalding water, then electrocuted.

The scent of frying flesh sticks to my clothes, and I must wash them immediately upon my return.

I can't eat chicken any longer.

I occasionally eat fish, but if I saw a fish processing plant I'm sure I wouldn't. I try not to think of such unpleasantries.

My father needs me to help him look over the books. He has people to do this for him, of course. However, my father still likes to think of his company as a family business. He refuses to use a computer—so this entails files, reading a lot of numbers and digits. His eyes are feeding on him. Bifocals are not enough.

We do this and then I'm hungry.

He offers to take me to a local grill, but we stop at a soup and salad place instead. I order lentil soup and greens.

WAIST

My father is thinning, shrinking, condensing. I know this happens in old age, but my father's case seems extreme.

He wears a size twenty-nine waist slacks. Sometimes we can only find these in the boys' section. He cinches his pants with a belt in which he has carved additional holes.

My waist seems to be increasing. Perhaps this is as a result of a lack of sexual interest. Nevertheless, it surprises me—I eat healthily, mostly vegetarian. I exercise.

I blame cheese—a guilty pleasure.

My father jogs five miles a day, every day. A day without jogging is, for my father, not a true day. I blame jogging for my father's twenty-nine inch waist.

THIGHS

Zachary is returning home—shockingly.

He e-mails me saying he "found some trouble," and that the country is forcing him to return to the states. He refuses to say what the trouble is.

Four days later he calls me, comes over. He is gaunt and weary and as scraggly as I've ever seen him. I feed him and he eats whatever I place in front of him.

I don't ask him about the trouble.

I let him nap in the sunroom. The sunlight forms a triangle on his back as he sleeps.

When he wakes it is dark and I'm making lasagna.

"It was a prostitute, if you want to know."

I raise my hand and wave him off.

"She was different. I…we had something beyond…"

"Zachary," I say. "When will you grow up?" I immediately regret that.

I just don't want to know. He tells me she had amazing thighs… and did….and she was especially…and I turn my mind from him. I go downstairs and watch the news. It is less depressing.

When I return upstairs, the lasagna is finished. I serve him a square.

"Father wants to see you," I say. And I don't regret that. I wish it were easier.

KNEECAPS

Zachary doesn't have a car, so I drive him to my father's old house. The renters are moving in and he wants my help. I hide myself in the upstairs hall bathroom. I paint and let them talk. It is simple.

All I can hear are murmurings—mostly Zachary. His voice is much harder, ironically.

About half an hour later I hear a knock on the door.

"Let's go," Zachary says. His eyes are batting back and forth. "Can we go now?"

I want to finish what I'm doing. That, and my place is twenty minutes away—even if I want to come back the driving is going to take a chunk out of my day.

"Okay," I say.

In the car Zachary tells me that our father read him the riot act—said he's cutting Zachary out, that he doesn't want to see him or speak to him, that if he were a Mafioso, he'd break Zachary's kneecaps.

"My *father* said this. Can you believe it?"

Zachary covers his head in the crook of his right arm, like a ten-year-old. He says he just wants to go back to Laos.

"That's not a good idea," I say.

"I know."

"Be the opposite of a rolling stone. You should gather moss. *Collect* it."

I drive fast, faster than usual.

Shin/ankle/heel

When we get home, we listen to Brian Eno and Zachary smokes pot. I pretend not to care.

"So, now what?"

We are in the sunroom. The windows are open and the wind gusts. There's a dog four houses up that barks incessantly.

"I'm going back. I'm sorry, I can't help myself." He pulls one leg underneath himself. He grabs at his ankle and kicks off his sandals. He says he is always barefoot in Laos.

"Aren't you afraid?"

He thinks about it. He doesn't look at me. "No, I have to deal with it," he says.

"Whatever trouble you had there is only going to be waiting for you," I say.

"I know. I'm not running away from it. It was a mistake to come back here."

"No, it's been good to see you."

"I know, that's true. There's nothing here for me anymore. I've built myself my own little kingdom somewhere else."

It hurts to hear him say that. I'm not a priority to him, or not a high one. What happened to flesh and blood? That means something to me.

"Come and visit me any time," he says.

"But I hate traveling," I say. "It's a lot of walking."

"You get used to it," he says. "You can get used to anything."

That sounds like something our father would say, I think. I think Zach knows it.

TOENAILS

When I wake in the middle of the night, I am struck by the clicking of my toenails on the floor. I think of myself as some kind of nocturnal animal.

I go to the fridge and drink a glass of milk standing in front of it. I eat a few ginger snaps. This usually works.

When I return to bed, I dream the three of us are together—eating dinner at a family restaurant. We are laughing and telling stories and reminiscing. Piled in front of us is a giant pile of clams and we are opening them with our bare hands and sucking the meat from them and tossing the shells on the floor of the restaurant. The waiters scuttle over and sweep them up and refill our water glasses. In the dream, a jazz band plays a lulling sax and brush drum piece. We are the only diners in the restaurant.

My father's smile is wide and relaxed and Zachary is healthy and wears a suit and tie, loosened just so.

I look out over the restaurant and through the far window I can see the ocean lapping gently against a rocky shore. Seagulls swoop down and rise again.

When I look back to my family, they are gone. I'm sitting there at the table alone, the mound of clams in front of me. I listen to the music and look at my feet. My toes glow in the half-light.

I'll do something someday, I think. Then I wake up.

A FRIEND OF THE WORLD

PEOPLE MAKE THINGS more complicated than necessary. Things aren't *complicated.* They're simple. Rule #twenty-seven—you try hard, you succeed. I buy it. I work it. I stay laser-like, and I'm golden. I stray, lose myself in what so-and-so is wearing or look up—big trouble. Cameras.

Rule #fourteen—just follow through. Which Chief says means do as you're told. Which means take the order and process it. Like a cook in a restaurant. I wouldn't be caught *dead.*

I'M GOOD. I believe that. Mr. Lannon says I'm "disciplined." Says it's a rare trait to have, someone my age. I'm studying criminology. For a reason. Other reasons too, but the main reason is I want to be a detective. Always liked the idea of tracking, hunting, figuring out the puzzle. That's the challenge—putting it all together.

The girl who sits next to me is always in her pocket texting her boys. Knuckles pumping fabric. By "boys" I mean friends, not boyfriends. So, she says. What do I know? She's *smoking.* It's in the eyes—pupils big as quarters, Caribbean blue. I'm a sucker for a pretty face. The rest don't even matter to me. When the face is pretty, the rest follows. And she's popping.

A nice smile is all I need.

WE'RE IN the Sporting Goods Store. Chief says he wants the RG 2s. All sizes. Tough because shoes are big, bulky. Ally is on watchdog, so she's all eyeballs. We're in the shadow by the pillar. Their electronic eyes can't go there. We've hit them before. Many times.

I'm snapping the alligator tags behind the pillar. It's like plastic crab legs. I got a dozen that one time. The sun. The wind. The pinging docks.

I get three pairs into my booster bag and three more in Ally's. Home Depot—since there's one adjacent. They think we must have a bunch of hammers and nails or some shit on top of the lining. We've got layers of sandpaper, paint brushes and paint samples. So, there you go.

Ally's a good sight. No snooping clerks or assistant managers say shit. We buy a can of racquetballs. Cashier says, "You find everything okay?"

"I think so, honey," I say. "Didn't we?"

"Yes, dear," Ally says. She's sucking on a Lifesaver, smacking her lips.

"You know, we forgot the primer," I say. Bullshit small talk is the best distracter. Chief learned us well.

"Oh, we did," Ally says, almost sarcastic.

The cashier drops the can of racquetballs in the bag, then the receipt.

What does he care? We could lift a kayak, and as long as he doesn't get reprimanded he's solid. Big Polynesian-looking guy with a wide face and gold earring in his right ear. Gives him the look of Mr. Clean, just a bit.

Me and Ally walk out slow, holding hands. This is the only part that gives me cramps. The detector. Chief says just to turn around and shrug shoulders. Cashiers are used to falsies and (again) don't really care anyway. The percents are in our favor, he says. But it doesn't happen. We walk right through, bags in the trunk and drive away. Nine hundred worth of shoes, cleancleanclean.

I IMAGINE Ally clothes-less. I don't have to. I don't exactly want her, so it goes. But still. You work with someone enough, you can get used to the idea. There are worse things to adjust to. Plus, she knows this side of me. Nobody else does, except the others Chief brought in. And Chief, of course.

He shows nothing when we drop the shoes off at the port. No smile. No thank you. This is how he does it. Keeps us craving approval. Just a little acknowledgement, something.

We line them up on the fold-out. It's all kinds of stuff. Watches, DVDs, deodorant, medications, knives, smart phones, lamps, clocks, soap, batteries, books, coffee, detergent. Everything jumbled together, no order. He shows nothing, gives nothing.

"I'll call you soon," he says. That "soon" is promising. That's about as close to a "good job" as I've received.

Don't let him down though. He'll tear you up.

Chief looks like an African warlord. And he's African. Rumor has it, from Cameroon. But others say Niger. He's not a nice man. He's not your friend. It's all business all the time. Money runs through his veins.

It's fine with me. Less complicated this way.

The fluorescents buzz and moths ping against them. It smells like cat piss in there. Always does, always will.

"HEY, MOM," I say. "Home."

She kisses my cheeks, says she couldn't wait until I come home. She spoils me like a grandmother would. I'm the youngest, so that could have something to do with it.

"I got you something," she says. As if today is different from any other. She's always giving me something.

She hands me a box. Says, Open it. It's RX2s, running shoes. I about crap myself, thinking she must know. Thinking it's a sign.

Thinking it's a subtle hint she's trying to send me. But when I watch her face, I don't see that in her. She's just trying to encourage me. Track, which is what I'm best at in life. Pure speed. When I'm working for Chief, I always know I can outrun any rent-a cop who might try to chase me down.

I'm hunting a cheetah. I close my eyes and I'm flying through the grass and the sun is warm against the back of my neck and I'm gaining on him. No human has run so fast before. I've got my RX2s and my mother is by the tree watching me fly, clapping her hands. I can hear her and the pounding of the cheetah as I gain on him. I can smell his tart sweat and the katydids in the grasses leap up as we run. Some thwack against my face. And.

"Do you like them?"

"Thanks, Mom. Yeah."

It's possible she's making up for everything before. Her guilt is an engine. It's okay though. I'll take it.

"That shit was tight," Ally says.

"I know, right?"

"It was like we were *invisible*. They didn't even *see* us."

"I know."

Chief glowers. We're sitting there in the back. The buzz is going from the fluorescents. Chief is drinking Red Bull and vodka, spitting sunflower seeds on the floor. Nobody is talking.

Chief just gave a speech about how we needed to "up the ante." More supply needed. We're constantly running out of product, he said. Who wouldn't want two gallons of Tide for five bucks? At the store it would be four times that.

"We're doing the people a service," he said. "You remember Robin the Hood, right? This shit is our Nottinghood Forest."

I *couldn't* correct him.

Ally calls him Neg Nan (Negative Nancy).

ALLY AND I are in the Gucci Giant—bigbigbig. This get is totally different. There are people everywhere. It's not like you can just slip anything in your pocket without looking. The razor blades and condoms are all behind glass anyway.

Chief wants Tide. If not Tide then Downy. If not Downy then the generic.

Ally has the shopping cart parked in the detergent aisle and I'm dropping two-gallon bottles in there, as many as we can squeeze in. Lady passes us, giving us a dirty look. Stringy lady with a rooster head. She looks back at us as if she knows. I think she might say something. But she doesn't.

The cart is heavy as shit. Ally can't push it. This is not a good start, I think.

"We both need to do it," I say.

Our car is parked around back.

"It's too heavy," she says.

So, we're pushing it toward the door, but dropping ballast as we go. Too much, too much. Three less and it feels as if we can go fast, which is what we want.

We pull up to the bulletin board next to the exit. No detector at all. I glance back and don't see anybody eyeballing. Could be a renta up in the ceiling on the cams. But I doubt it. Not at a grocery store.

I slowly nose it in the right direction. Ally edges next to me.

I whisper. "One. Two. Three."

We push as fast as we can right out the automatic. We're flying past the old ladies on the sidewalk, nearly knock over a girl collecting donations. I've never pushed so fast in my life. Those new treads work like a charm.

"Wait," I hear behind us. I don't stop to find out.

We turn the corner, race down the sidewalk. Ally pops the doors. We are hurling the detergent in, two at a time. Someone is yelling.

She hops around and in. I slide in back. A cashier is churning after us, outfit flailing. But it's too late—we crash the cart and peel out of there.

We're laughing. We get a few miles off, duck onto a side street. At the light I kiss her. My tongue and her tongue. She flushes and smacks the steering wheel. We turn up the ska. It's all she listens to and I'm happy to go along. I pound along on the dashboard.

MR. GANNON is talking about borderline cases. He says if law was cut and dry, it wouldn't change. He says law is dynamic and enforcement of it is constantly evolving, changing, mutating. He says it's like an organism.

He brings up the example of student cheating.

"We all know plagiarism is wrong, but is it 'illegal,' per se? Not really. You can't be *arrested* for plagiarism. You can't even be arrested for being one of those guys who runs the plagiarizing websites. You can help hundreds of students all over America cheat and you're safe. Is that right?"

"No," I say. "If it was it wouldn't feel wrong? Not that I know from experience.

Laughing. Ethics.

"A feel, good. Interesting point about the role of intuition. Has anyone done something wrong that they later feel guilty about?"

I don't say anything.

I wish Ally was here. She's harder than me, more able to shoot down ideas she doesn't like.

Nobody says anything. Tough question to get a response to.

Borderline. Who isn't on some kind of border or another?

CHIEF HANDS ME an extra ten.

"Good," he says. He means the Tide.

I nod. This is a loud thank you for him. I exhale. Praise accepted.

"It's hard," he says. "Grocery, very tough."

I nod. It's a great day.

I NEVER hear back from Ally. She doesn't text me. Nothing.

It's Jess and Felix and Paul and me. We're eating candy corn even though its spring. Felix found them in the back. They taste sour or something, and I'm wondering if candy corn can go bad.

He has the others hit another grocery, different part of town. He says I've earned my solo.

"You know what 'lollygag' means?"

"No," I say.

"Go casual." He means the mall.

"Lollygag" means a "friendly." Not friendly like I'm out to make friends. Have to be smart, not take anything easy. It means I pick what I want. This takes the pressure off.

I can't stand the mall. Too many kids my age I might bump into, too much boomboomboom in the eye. I walk past Victoria's Secret. All that cleavage and fuck-me stares—too much. Easier going to the family stores. I remember there used to be an arcade on one of the side corridors. Gone now—everything has their hour. I duck into the religious bookstore—only one in the mall. I'm leafing through books telling me how to follow Jesus, how to live saintly, how to eat Christian, how to feel right about the world. The nice leather Bibles are up front. I never knew so many different kinds. The Bibles are *popping*. Brown Bibles. Red Bibles. Black Bibles. I like the black Bible with the gold cross. It looks like the kind you could swear an oath on, for real. Something even the Pope might carry.

There's no detector, so I carry it to my side down the back. It's just one orange haired black lady with a nice smile, me, and a couple with kids. Orange Hair is reading an *Us Weekly*. In back it's incense and greeting cards. I slip the good book down my pants. My jacket obscures it. Easy peasy. I walk right out. Orange Hair doesn't even look up from her gossip crap.

Out in the mall I'm in the food court. I flip it open—random page.

"What causes quarrels and causes fights among you? Is it not this—that your passions are at war within you? Do you not know that friendship with the world is enmity with God? Therefore whoever wishes to be a friend of the world makes himself an enemy of God."

Shit, man. Think.

I walk through the crowds, still thinking. What am I doing with the life I've been given? I haven't done anything. It's not even about right or wrong. I know I won't mess around with this forever. But I should at least live well. With quality.

I duck into the candy store. Every mall has one. I bag up a bunch of my favorites and just fucking bolt. I got the Bible in one hand and a bag in the other. I can't go wrong. Except a kid in his candy cane outfit is behind me. I'm faster than him though, I can tell. If I just keep bolting, he'll give up. I'm weaving in and out, knocking bags away.

"Hey, asshole!" I speed up. The new shoes help, that little extra grip. I can feel my leg muscles twitch in ecstasy. I'm *enjoying* this. I turn my head and he's further back. I bolt into Macy's. I'm running faster than I've ever run before. Perfume. Ladies'. Men's. Upstairs. Juniors. Sportswear. Kitchen. Bathroom. Furniture. My insides are *whirling*. I duck behind an armoire and count. There's no way he's even on this floor, I think.

I count to a hundred and don't hear anybody. I slip into the bathroom. I stand on the toilet seat and eat my gummy worms and wait. Nothing. He lost the trail.

I wait ten more minutes and then walk out, still counting candy.

That's when I feel the two hands on my shoulder. Guy with bleached-blonde hair and a savage look. Looks like that Rutger whatever guy in that movie Mr. Gannon made us watch. The robot.

"You're in a world of trouble, asswipe."

I just freeze. I stand there and he stands there, his paws clutching me. I don't look up.

He has to be mall renta. Couldn't be Macy's. They wouldn't have enough dogs in the race.

"The time for thinking was yesterday," he says. "Where are your parents?"

"I'm nineteen," I say.

"Like I said, where are your *parents*?"

He jabs me in the back with his finger.

"Let's you and me go in the back."

I DON'T SAY anything about Chief. I don't say anything about anything. I have to eat that shit. I know it.

I said the Bible is mine—luckily, I had peeled off the sticker already. So, it's a bag of candy. They can't do shit for that. But he writes me up anyway, hands me the pink copy. It's like I'm getting fired from life. It won't be anything though. Judge won't even look at it, and I'll just have to suck up the court fees. That's it.

Ironic. I wasn't even doing anything and I get caught. I bet the renta keeps the candy for his fat ass.

I don't tell chief, Ally, nobody. The less they know about everything the better. I'm done with this. It's just when.

I LAY LOW. For about a week I watch television and eat popcorn.

Chief asks where I've been.

"School."

"Some lame excuse, my friend."

Whenever somebody says "buddy" or "my friend" it means the exact opposite.

Rule #thirteen from Chief. Perfect your practice. He likes to twist things inside out, but the meaning is the same.

Ally looks at me.

He sends us back to the sporting goods. This time—golf balls. Nothing but as many golf balls as we can get. Back to the booster bags.

This time there's an old plain-clothes following us. Comb over. I see him right off and nudge Ally. We're looking at the golf balls, but this guy is eyeballing us like-we're made of bacon.

"727," I say.

Code for abort operation. Rule #twenty-two—pick your battles.

We walk in. We're in the back. I like checking out the "outdoor zone"—tents and kayaks and backpacks. They have a kayak. Ally and I get in it. She's up front, I'm in back. We take the paddles and we're rowing.

The plainclothes is just standing there. Picking at a scab or something.

It's the Mississippi and we're flowing down into the lowlands. Cranes are lifting off as we paddle. Cattails are bobbing along the shore. We wave to the guys fishing and the ladies in the powerboat. The sun is out and I ask Ally if she needs more sunscreen. I drink from the cool water. It's refreshing and endless. Her eyes in my eyes. I can see my reflection in each pupil.

We have a long way to go and our energy is boundless.

HURRY UP AND RELAX

☞

WE DON'T *really* know Paulie, but we love Paulie. Who doesn't? He's a model citizen, in most respects. He holds a job, pays his taxes, drives American (and who wants to do *that*?). He is compassionate towards animals, loves children. He takes care of the elderly. He donates to the right charities. Paulie's problem isn't lack of love—though lack of sex might be a contributing factor. We wouldn't know about that. His problem is lack of self-love. He doesn't take care of himself properly. He needs training. He eats crap. He rarely, if ever, exercises. He weighs eighty pounds more than he should and his sleeping habits are abysmal—too many margaritas, too much time spent in front of the computer role-playing (the blue glow at 2:36 a.m., we see it).

We worry.

But it's okay. He's Paulie. When we aren't worrying, we look up to him. He is better than us. We know he will ultimately win out.

He told us he's fried—too much work, nothing but work. Where has all the time gone? He wondered aloud. He wondered if he would collapse at his desk, his mouse in hand, a Super-Sized Pepsi sweating next to his bruised head.

He needed to "smell the roses."

So, staycation, he said. He just wanted time away from the office, time to be in the place he most liked to be.

"It's a shit box, I know," he said. Paulie is underwater. He bought at the height of the market, the bubbliest part of the bubble. He can never sell, not until it's paid off twenty-three years from now. His shit box is his financial prison cell. And if his shit box is his prison cell, he's going to fix it up the best he can. He's going to care for it.

Swirled his finger in a margarita. Licked his finger clean.

"I just want to be home for a week, take care of things around the house. Relax, breathe deeply. Zen-out, you know."

We get it. We nod with strong affirmation.

"I want to hurry up and relax. Blow off work, cash-in vacation time."

"Do it," we said. "We want you to." We only had Paulie's welfare in mind.

DAY 1

Paulie noodled around the house, inspecting this, inspecting that.

Jesus, he thought—this place is breaking apart at the seams. The little shed out back was decomposing, the bathroom sorely needed a new paint job; overhead lights needed updating; something was wrong with the clattering ceiling fan; the A.C. needed servicing. There are probably a hundred other small things he couldn't even see. We watched him pace around his home, probing. We were home owners, also. We knew Paulie's apprehension.

He clicked on Craigslist and sent e-mails. A few guys responded but seemed sketchy or too expensive or fly-by-night or flaky. One guy responded—a Lans Fill. The name made Paulie chuckle and, subconsciously or not, perhaps he let his guard down as a result. He didn't believe the name for one second—neither did we. "Lans'" posting read: "Interested in job. Reasonable rats (sic). Competint (sic). Can start wenever (sic)." How Paulie was suckered by this we will never know.

On the phone "Lans" sounded folksy is all, more intelligent than his message would indicate, but with a touch of Georgia twang mixed with New Jersey or something. Somehow the mix came out alien. We'd heard it all before, but not *this*.

"I'm a jack of all trades, but my name happens to be Lans. So easy to remember." Hahahahahaha. Hahahahaha.

"Yeah," Paulie said. "I have a bunch of things for you to do. When can you come by and get started? I mean, at your convenience. I don't want to put you out or nothing."

"Well, that's the odd part about all of this, isn't it?"

"What's odd?" Still wary.

"I'm going to need a ride."

"You're kidding, right? You don't have a *car*?" What kind of contractor doesn't have a car? Even warier, we know.

At this point, we believed Paulie should have bailed immediately, found another guy—handymen being as common as weeds. Should have listened to his intuition. But Paulie was stubborn. Once he squirreled an idea into his head he wanted to see it through, even if the idea was a poor one. It left him with a sense of completion. He liked the feeling of having a mission.

"Okay, fine," Paulie said. "I will give it a shot." They arranged a place. The guy's rates *were* decent—that was something. It would balance out, Paulie thought. We weren't so sure. We were wary, wary for Paulie.

Day 2

We knew "Lans" would be late, and he was. Paulie stood around for half an hour, cell phone in hand, pacing up and down the sidewalk outside of the Metro. Fifteen minutes later, "Lans" still hadn't shown up. About ready to throw in the towel, a giant string bean of a man slumped out of the corridor and bent forward to greet our Paulie.

"Are you Paulie, by any chance?"

"That's me. Where *were* you, man?"

"My deepest, most sincere apologies," "Lans" said. "I was delayed by circumstances outside of my control."

"And what would those be? Those circumstances?"

"Circumstances, you know? Circumstances. I couldn't help. Unavoidable as shit."

Paulie was not sure what that meant.

"Fine," Paulie said, eventually.

"Lans" sighed. "Let's go, no?"

Paulie led the way to his car. It was hot and sticky and the pollen made Paulie cough. We felt for him—it bothered us, too. It likely bothered us more than it bothered him.

Paulie worried that "Lans" was too tall to sit in the car. Then he noticed that "Lans" was empty-handed.

"Hey, where are your tools?"

"Well, that's the odd part, isn't it?"

"Let me guess—you don't have tools?"

"Lans" scrunched his face into a shamefaced sack.

"I was hoping maybe we could take a trip to the hardware store and pick up what we need. Things like that."

Paulie couldn't believe this guy. No car, no tools and shows up late. Even more than that, he couldn't believe his own stupidity for going with him in the first place. So many other options. We tried to tell him. Paulie was the opposite of impulsive, but everyone has an off day.

But since he had committed, he didn't have much of a choice but to stick it out.

"Ok, fine," Paulie said. "Let's just go."

The faster Paulie purchased whatever "Lans" needed, the quicker his staycation could commence. We hoped it would begin immediately. Paulie deserved it, we knew. We wanted to see a relaxing Paulie.

"Lans" was too tall to sit in the front of Paulie's little shit box Yaris, so he relaxed in the backseat, his knees jutting upward. Paulie looked back at "Lans"—Paulie felt as if he were the chauffeur.

At the hardware store, "Lans" seemed lost. Paulie described in minute detail the various jobs "Lans" would be doing, but "Lans" said he was trying to "visualize" what he needed. Paulie just purchased anything he thought he might need—no sense in scrimping on his house at this point. He spent $350 on two baskets of tools and supplies. He tried to look at the positive side—he'd certainly need these tools later, wouldn't he? We knew he wouldn't, or not enough to make it worthwhile. We said nothing.

Day 3

Paulie had "Lans" spend the night, which concerned us, because what was happening to his staycation? He was allowing the home projects to consume him. Paulie was out in the ratty cul-de-sac in front of his house complaining: "Lans" won't wake up now—he drank one too many bogarted margaritas—and Paulie, as a result, worried that "Lans" had no idea what he was doing. This was the larger concern. We offered our help if he needed to contact the Better Business Bureau or throw the guy back to the street. We would play the role of house bouncer, if needed.

"He's nine feet tall," Paulie said. "He could eat all of us for breakfast."

Paulie fretted far too much. We reminded him of this. He worried about the stove, about the coffee maker. He worried about the unlocked door, about his computer contracting a virus, about his car brakes abruptly failing. He took pills for panic attacks at one point (we wondered if he maybe ceased this practice too hastily). He ate standing up over the sink, usually, food debris falling onto the dirty dishes.

Paulie frequently acted as if one foot was out the door. Paulie acted as if a car sat idling on the curb, waiting for him. His head was elsewhere.

So "Lans" slept in. Paulie tried nicely, then not so nicely—to rouse him. He didn't budge. By eleven thirty, "Lans" rolled over. Paulie at this point sat a territorial vigil by "Lans'" bedside.

"Hey, man, come on. Time to help me. Get up."

Paulie thought "Lans" was faking it, but "Lans" explained it was a sleep disorder—associated with narcolepsy, something related to his height, slow metabolism. Paulie fed him, caffeinated him. Paulie talked him through the jobs. They agreed that "Lans" would start with the painting, move to electrical work, then finish off repairing the shed. Paulie had to call someone else for the A.C., he knew that.

"I'll be upstairs if you need anything," Paulie said.

This, he thought, was the beginning of his staycation proper. Now he could rest. Let "Lans" do the work.

But rest was impossible. He tried to read a magazine and couldn't sit still for more than five minutes. He tried to calm his thoughts, but his mind raced to the several other thousand things he could be doing. He paced. On the computer he checked this and that, then realized he was working again, still working despite his staycation, so he returned to the arm chair and the magazine. But then ten minutes later he thought of something else he should check, something else he needed to attend to. Then the computer again.

Eventually Paulie wore himself out enough that he *had* to fall asleep—but it took some major doing.

Paulie woke up to the scent of something burning. He ran downstairs and "Lans" was prostrate on the floor in the kitchen with the overloaded fixture smoking.

"Jesus," Paulie said. He bolted downstairs, hit the circuit breaker and clomped back upstairs with the fire extinguisher.

Please don't let him be deceased, Paulie thought. Please don't let him be deceased. We knew Paulie must have been extremely nervous. Beyond wary. We were, and we were only watching, listening, ruminating.

Luckily "Lans" wasn't dead. He sat up straight, shaking out the cobwebs.

"First of all—are you okay?"

"I think so." "Lans" swatted at his head and shrugged.

"Why didn't you cut the breaker before you started working on the fixture? You could have killed yourself, Lans. You could have burnt the house down. Jesus."

"Lans" moved upwards and forward into a kneeling position. He shrugged and said this was the first time he tried one of these jobs. He had always been afraid of all the wires, he said.

"You've never done electrical work? Your ad said you did. Certification and all that."

"I mean I've replaced the things that protect the wall gashes. I think that counts."

"Jesus."

We wished Paulie didn't use the Lord's name in vain so frequently. It was below him. We guessed that "Lans" thought the same thing.

"I'm not paying you for this—in fact, you're going to pay *me* for damages."

"Lans" shrugged.

"Either way."

"Lans" crouched and shook his head as if to knock water from his ear canal. His half-baked thoughts, unfortunately stayed put.

"Are you even legit? Why should I keep you on?"

Paulie was saying the things he only previously thought. He was stepping up, being a man. We were so proud.

Then the sad sack story begins. "Lans" is the son of a nurse and a banker. He grows up in spoiled, suburban bliss. At age eleven when "Lans" is spending the night at a friend's house—his parents and little sister are all killed in a house fire (the authorities blamed the chimney). "Lans" is raised by his grandparents who are capable but old and "Lans" is haunted by the death of his family (he still isn't over it). He has trouble concentrating. He struggles academically and though he graduates high school, he bumps around odd jobs, works temporary gigs, waits tables, bartends. He doesn't find himself. He wouldn't admit to the bullshit Craigslist name. Paulie though—Paulie is, on some level, moved.

"Still haven't, truth be told," "Lans" said.

Just my luck, Paulie thought. I get the handyman with a midlife crisis.

Among other things.

DAY 4

The bathroom isn't bad. Let's start with that. We wouldn't have picked slate grey for the walls, but that was Paulie's decision—he's partial to silvers, greys, gunmetal. Paulie liked high ceilings and unencumbered floor plans (his ceilings are, in fact, not high; and he has far too much furniture cluttering the walking areas).

"Lans" woke up at noon. Considering Paulie didn't have to spend the time shuttling "Lans" to the E.R., he felt fortunate. We knew Paulie felt a touch generous, also. The good Samaritan, always.

In the light of the afternoon, even the bathroom was well-done. Paulie told him so.

"I've had more experience painting than anything else. I painted a lot right after high school. Thank you for the compliment."

Paulie was still hoping he could sneak some vacation time, cut his losses, hurry up and relax while there was still time. Pronto.

"Forget about the electrical work, obviously," Paulie said. "Just focus on the shed. Can you do that?"

"Lans" nodded. Paulie had an electrician coming over and an A.C. guy. One more day of "Lans" and then three more days of staycation without having to worry about house shit any longer. That's the part he really looked forward to—the post-"Lans" era. He really wasn't planning on having to hold "Lans'" hand throughout the process, but now that he was in this situation, he wanted to see it through to its natural resolution. He was stuck. By that point he really didn't care if "Lans" did a good job with the shed—he just wanted him gone. He'd give him a thousand bucks to just vamoose.

The A.C. guy and the electrician were a dream to work with compared with ramshackle "Lans." On time, quick, professional, reliable. They had tools—we saw them. They were competent. "Lans," on the other hand, stared at the shed as if Paulie asked him to perform a post-mortem heart operation on a just-discovered Neanderthal encased in ice.

Paulie stood at the rickety threshold of his shit box, surveilling. "Lans" pressed against the rotting plywood with one long finger and sniffed. We didn't care for his curled lip or his squinting eye.

"Looks a little soft," he said.

We knew Paulie must have been deeply apoplectic, usually he's a good sport; he's patient—clearly—more than we would be in his shoes. Far more.

"Lans" nodded.

"Can you fix it?"

"I don't know. It looks pretty rotten to me."

Paulie calmly said that's why we have the two by fours; that's why we have the plywood. That's why we have the roofing material. You rip out the old, put up the new. That's what this job entails.

"Lans" wriggled his finger into the rotting wood. Paulie watched this.

"I'll help you," Paulie said. "It's okay."

And that afternoon Paulie showed "Lans" how to do the job. They knocked the old plywood out with a sledgehammer—Paulie did. They removed the old doors, the old hinges. Paulie showed

"Lans" how to nail up the new plywood, how to screw on new hinges. They painted—Paulie knew "Lans" could handle that. By 7:00 p.m. they were finished.

"You did the work. I was just the helper," "Lans" said.

"We start somewhere."

They went inside, showered. Paulie made some food—fried chicken and corn. They watched the game. "Lans" fell asleep in the blue glow. I could be friends with this guy, Paulie thought. I'd never hire him again, but we could be buds.

Let the record state that we did not approve.

Day 5

On the drive back to the Metro "Lans" was contrite.

"I don't know what I was thinking," "Lans" said. "I'm not handy. I don't know what I'm doing. I'm just a guy trying to survive. On a whim really." He started to tear up. Please. Please. No tears—there's no crying in contract work.

"It's okay, dude," Paulie said. He had already waved the white flag. He handed "Lans" a wad of money—the agreed upon price. "You'll figure it out." He considered it a life donation.

There was something about "Lans" that reminded Paulie of his grandfather—the doe-eyed passivity, the sweet disposition beneath the crusty layers. Try as he might, Paulie couldn't stay angry at the guy. We would have differed in this regard. At any rate, now his stay-cation could finally commence. Couldn't it?

"Lans" and Paulie shook hands. We knew Paulie felt a deep sense of relief that the house was even standing. "Lans's" walk back to the Metro station initially seemed slumped and downtrodden, but when he honked the horn in a friendly goodbye, "Lans" lifted his head and his bearing.

Paulie will give the guy a call down the road to check in—an easy prediction.

Alone in his shit box at last! Paulie's house seemed to groan. His cat, Fidel, came out from hiding, clicking around *his* shit box. Paulie tried to unwind—video games, music, beer. He called his brother. He paced back and forth, wired still. Jittery. Pacing. Pacing. Paulie was not sure why. He hoped he someday would land a lady—someone to calm him down, if nothing else. He paced like a trapped animal. He stood over the sink and ate a burrito and two bananas. Then he paced some more.

We knew his state. We too could not relax. We too felt compelled to do, to think, to process. We too were driven by some invisible motor, always churning.

Paulie worried about "Lans" now. His mind was now where "Lans" was. The guy was a sinking ship, Paulie could see that. Paulie kneaded his forehead. That "Lans."

Eventually, Paulie exhausted himself and collapsed in front of the television. This was a good thing. He reclined in the spot where "Lans" fell asleep earlier. It was a comfortable spot, Paulie thought. We hoped he slept tight, that he would find solace.

Paulie wondered what "Lans'" real name was. He should have asked. *Why* didn't he ask? Tristan York? Yancy Bell? Bobby Plinton? Peter Nester? Nick Oglethorpe? Oscar White? Paulie wondered how many guesses it would take to get it? What is the possible combination of names? It's not infinite.

Maybe, we thought, Paulie would just call the guy and ask. If he even answered his phone. He might not, we knew.

We hoped Paulie realized how much he did have—that's usually the most difficult realization of all. In the morning though he paced again, knee bobbling, arms twitching, eyes widening. The car was running outside. We could almost hear it.

DROP

☞

Day 2

"Jesus did not walk on water," I say. "You know that, right? It was ice. Read an article. There was a cold snap, chunks of ice right there in the Middle East."

"Oh, don't be ridiculous," she says. She massages my knee, plants a peck on my check. "It's okay, He'll forgive you for saying that."

"How about a real job instead?"

10,000 envelopes sit in white boxes stacked on the floor. We're yanking them from the stack one-by-one, sliding the blue and orange Mountain Brook Resort mailer into each one, applying the address sticker. I'm on flyer detail. She gets the stickers—easier job. We save the sealing for the end.

"We're working right now," she says. "We should be grateful."

"Grateful for what exactly? We're *envelope* stuffers."

"It's something. It's good for now. It's money in the bank as long as we don't make a bonfire."

"Correction," I say. "It's *cents* in the bank."

Knee massage again with a hint of sarcastic tickle. This means she wants me to shut the fuck up. But nicely.

It's not a bad motel exactly. It's just a bit crumbly—a Tastkykake version of a real motel. The bathroom seems relatively clean for a dive. We heard it was better than it seemed from the outside. For our seventh motel in the past two months I'd say it's somewhere in the middle of the pack.

At five I'm done with the stuffing. We count 6,550 completed, which equals $65.50 for the day. Minus $43.24 and dinner (Wendy's), we may save ten or eleven dollars.

"Every bit counts," she says. We're eating hamburgers.

"No, it doesn't," I say. "We may as well be indentured servants."

DAY 7

Losing 1760 Willowcrest wasn't the worst thing in the world. At least at that juncture the mortgage monkey was off our back for good. Regret is the real demon. I'm sitting on the "comforter" on our queen-sized, looking at the purple and blue and red swirly pattern on it, trying to decide (1) who came up with this hideous monstrosity and (2) why did the White Crescent Motel choose *this* particular hideous pattern rather than any of the other possible (*less?*) hideous patterns at their disposal and (3) was there a committee?

A committee is exactly what I needed back in 2008—some team to save me (and us) from myself. Instead, we bought at the peak and suffered like chumps. We're not unique.

It didn't help that I was a "consultant." People used to toss that word around gleefully (Frisbee-like), with a sense of braggadocio. "Consultant" equaled someone giving two shits about what you think and paying for it. Now we realize it means jack. "Consultant" might as well equal "freelancer."

I got nothing. Nada.

We're in a routine of taking our "continental breakfast" gratis in the little "breakfast nook" of the White Crescent. This means de-thawed mini-bagels and spotted bananas with a side coffee so thin you can see the bottom of the Styrofoam fucking cup that may or may not include non-dairy creamer (I'm afraid to investigate the chemical makeup of that). Occasionally, White Crescent splurges for individually wrapped (dry) mini-muffins—the kind you find at 7-11 next to the day-old donuts. Or sometimes they spring for some orange colored version of orange juice (but it's not Tang and it's definitely not orange juice—just orange dye and sugar). We snag a couple extra bagels and cream cheese samples for lunch.

I like to get down there by eight to avoid the ruckus; she's not in a hurry and likes the social scene—as it were—at any rate. Seven days in and she's everybody's best friend.

I don't care. Give me my preservatives, food coloring and paltry caffeine injection and let me hole back in my room and stuff envelopes until my fingers bleed and my wife scolds me gently, again, for using the Lord's name in vain (while in the next breath mentioning that He will forgive my sins, He being the God of all compassion and understanding—good to have him on my side).

We need to purchase some rubber gloves before we run out of Band-Aids. My fingers are in tatters.

Day 12

I'm hacking and coughing so much. The dust mites or whatnot causing this are receiving the workout of their lives—climbing into, and then rapidly finding themselves expelled from, my respiratory system. This gives me serious pause. She's on both knees in front of the calypso comforter praying for a respite (for me) from the allergens. When we run the window fan, it helps.

I have yet to find my bloody lungs splayed on the comforter. Matters could be worse. As a sidebar, I'm sure these are not the only disgusting body fluids which have been spewed all over this comforter. I've read the articles. I read articles. We might as well take a wad of used toilet paper, smear it all over the toilet and sleep on that. And yet, we still used the comforter anyway, like morons. We'll probably get Ebola from this blanket.

"I wonder if...." She starts.

"It's too late for this," I say. At eight-thirty my middle-aged brain is fried and I'm ready to dissolve into myself. It's eight-seventeen.

"There's nothing wrong with Pennsylvania," she says. "We can stuff there, too."

"I like it here," I say. "It's not bad."

"You don't sound good."

"It'll ease up. It could be stress. Stress makes it worse."

We have the weather channel going in the background. The screen is showing images of drought staining the Midwest—a big blotch of dryness.

"We could start anew," she says. "There's nothing wrong with a clean start."

I don't respond. I lean back into a stack of three pillows and close my eyes. I regret every stupid meaningless lunch and flat screen purchase and asinine music download and trip to the Outer Banks. I recall one particular dinner at this expensive Italian place in the city. We just kept ordering appetizer after unnecessary appetizer, bottles of wine, lavish desserts—all of it. Why? The bill came to something like $680 for four people. It was something else.

Day 14

The coughing has subsided with an assist from the maids (we tipped them $20 with the promise that they vacuum everything three times over, *please, pretty please*).

She has taken to visiting Earl and Kitty in 237 and or Bud and Jocelyn or Aunt Dot—this is what Aunt Dot calls herself, at least. Or they crash into our room.

We didn't know White Crescent Motel had the reputation for collecting castaways. In college I was Phi Beta Kappa. That meant something to me then. The underground is news to me.

Earl and Kitty come over and they drink a twelve pack of whatever cheap brew is on sale at Kurt's Konvenience down the block. Then they run their mouths. Kitty says she lives for drinking and television. This strikes me as possibly the saddest thing I've ever heard.

They were both in real estate.

I tell her it's exhausting having Earl and Kitty over, but she thinks the two of them are just misplaced souls in need of guidance.

When she pays for them at night, she asks the Lord if they could please cease and desist with the alcohol consumption. I ask her if she thinks her prayers are going to make a whit of difference.

"It can't hurt."

We come from opposite perspectives on this.

Bud and Jocelyn are depressives, which gives me hope because at least they have wised up. They have little to offer conversationally, however. When we run out of things to talk about (which is often fifteen minutes in), they sing for us. Gospely/bluesy songs. Sometimes Jocelyn plays the banjo in accompaniment. She was a lawyer a few years back. He was an accountant. Now they do spot temp work, when they can get it.

And they live in this shit hole, too.

Aunt Dot likes to dispense advice.

"You two should quit it," she says, referring to the envelope packing. "Go to Littleton, Arkansas. That's where the new Dowdell plant is going to be. Get your roots in the ground there and pretty soon you'll have your life all over again."

Aunt Dot doesn't care for the others. She wears flowing ex-hippie wear and fifteen bangles on each wrist. Her hair looks like kelp.

"She's an old soul," my wife says.

"She's an old something," I say.

Day 19

I have so many paper cuts on my fingers they are entirely wrapped in tape and Band-Aids. I look like a boxer. All for one cent per envelope for Mountain Brook Resort. As we stuff the envelopes, I wonder how many recipients of their flyer (A) Read it and (B) Think their free-weekend sounds like a good fucking idea or (C) Care about a trip to middle-of-the-swamp Florida. I'd say .001 percent, if MBR is lucky. And this .001 percent most likely consists of the senile or schizophrenic who don't know any better. The whole thing stinks—it's either a total scam or a cult or a drug thing, or maybe all of the above.

Goddamn, I think. What am I doing? I just want to sleep.

"Don't you worry now," she says. I'm half-asleep, face pressed into a pillow. "I believe in us. Everything is going to be fine."

Somehow, despite the saccharine tang of all of it, she still does make me feel better.

"Holy smokes, if you weren't propping me up, who would?"

She's patting my back.

I married Mother Theresa.

I look around at the tacky motel art.

I once had a great job and house. Now, nothing.

When I walk I walk slowly, as if it were 500 degrees outside. I'm filled with dread.

"I don't know," she says. "I guess you'd be left to the wolves in your mind."

"How can you possibly retain such optimism? How do you *do* it?"

She smiles and shrugs and cuts the lights. She knows I know it was a stupid question, though she'd never call it that. She hums to me as I drift off, patting my back.

"It will all work out," she hums.

Day 27

I'd love to vanish—disappear to some obscure country where the creditors can't touch me. I used to believe I had to live in America otherwise I wouldn't be "in touch" with what's going on. Now, everything is online anyway. And America isn't America anymore.

I just want a better me.

She doesn't believe in divorce, as if divorce were some kind of mythological creature—the Loch Ness monster or Abominable Snowman.

I don't hold anything against her. I'm simply ashamed of our situation. It would be easier if I didn't feel responsible.

We stuff envelopes for hours in near silence. I wouldn't call it inspiring. I'm tired after an hour, but I keep going. Every finger is bandaged and I still keep going.

When I'm not stuffing, I notice I move even slower, as if burdened by heat stroke.

I have a recurring nightmare that I will die with a stack of envelopes between my legs, a flyer in each hand. What a joke.

DAY 33

They're all there—Bud and Jocelyn, Aunt Dot, Earl and Kitty. Also, some newbies—Salvadorians and Hondurans who are unsure if they are going to attempt to return back to their home country or seek another paltry gig in some other town. It's bad here.

I'm tired of eating hard potato rolls.

When she's asleep tomorrow I'm going to make my move.

We're sitting there eating our toasted bagels with jam and drinking Styrofoam cup after Styrofoam cup of weak coffee. It's better than nothing.

There's a guy who says he knows of a warehouse which is hiring down route 56 all the way out near the chicken farms. He says the pay is pretty decent, all things considered and that it's guaranteed for three weeks, minimum. They have rush orders to fill. They have cats in the basement—and a cafeteria.

From my position this sounds incredible.

I smile at her as she chats up her friends and I hold her hand under the table. I squeeze it. She must know in her heart of hearts how I feel—how dismal it is right now for me. How I had to pawn off my comic book collection just to scrounge enough money to be where I am now.

I'm looking out the window. It is still hot and dusty and dry. We live in a rain shadow. I can't remember the last time it rained.

If I could live in the shower stall I would.

Day 34

She's on her knees, her hands clasped on the bed. She's mouthing words of prayer. I know she's desperately thinking of me.

She opens her eyes and stands, says we should get going to breakfast.

"Go on without me today," I say.

She shoots me a quizzical look—it says both that I need the energy and that I should be more social. Even if she doesn't say it, I know she wants me to reach out more to the others. "Reaching out" is about the last thing I'd like to do.

"Bring me back some stuff, okay?"

The door clicks behind her.

I wonder how things would be different if my mother were alive. I bet I wouldn't be so clingy. I bet I would've left a long time before.

That night she's reading next to me. I can barely close my eyes. All I can think about is what's next. I pretend to read an old *National Geographic* someone left in the room, but all I can do is glance at the pictures.

When she eventually snaps the reading lamp off, I listen to her breathing slow. When I know she's asleep I place my arm over her torso, I can feel her warmth. I stay in that position for a long time.

And then I lift my body, bit by bit.

EXACT CHANGE

THE GUY with the hat that says "head." He wears clothes to remind him of which part of the body it is supposed to cover? His interior is a dusty mess. The upholstery is grimy, smeared. The dashboard is sticky with dust and residue. Even the change he hands me is gritty, as if a volcano spewed ash inside his car. He waits. I count it. He nods. No words. I swear, filth seems to chuff off in the wind as he drives off.

Is it my imagination or does he cross himself?

I'm boothing again today, cash line. Lines twenty cars long. Tempers short. It's July.

THE LADY driving the chicken truck hands me a dollar bill.

"Exact change only," I tell her.

"Cripes, I'm sorry, amigo."

"Tell me a story, and I'll let you pass."

She pauses, looks in the rearview. Slight smile.

"I picked up a hitchhiker once who swore Otis Redding was still alive. You know who he is, right? Otis, I mean."

I've heard of him, but don't know really. I nod anyway. I like the name Otis though. Canine.

"This hitchhiker I picked up once said he met Otis Redding outside of a Dumpster, picking old apples from a garbage bag."

"'Is your name Otis?' the guy asked."

"'I'm just sittin' here restin' my bones,' he said, and wandered off into the dusky sky."

"The hitchhiker later stole my pocket book, though it only had thirty bucks and no credit cards. So I'm not sure I believed him. Took me forever to straighten out the license."

I let her through. Nice story, even if it was just a story. She winked.

I HATE when people don't even say "hi" or "thank you." One or the other is all I ask for. How much time or energy does it take to utter one or two syllables? A second? You don't have one second to spare? Make somebody's day a touch nicer. This one lady does the I'm-not-going-to-acknowledge-you thing. I don't let her though. Say she owes another quarter. She argues but ultimately gives in. That's right, you acknowledge me now, don't you? If she was nice, I'd be nice. It would be nice.

IT'S A HOT and humid day, but *moderately* hot, moderately humid. I've done much worse. There are days it's so muggy I sweat continually. The world seems *made* of sweat on those days.

Even on a moderately hot and humid day the drivers will say: "Stay cool!"

I nod.

Stay cool. Easy to say when *you've* got A/C and I don't. They mean well, though. They're thinking of me, if only for a moment.

There are days I wish I was *wearing* an air conditioner.

IT'S NOT a bad job and it pays better than you think. Benefits are solid, actually. It opens my eyes, seeing all kinds. I've seen ladies giving birth, people in full intimacy embrace in the back, a guy holding his arm in a tourniquet rushing to the hospital. A compact stuffed with twelve people. Drugs, and everything. God knows how many psychopaths I've encountered. I've been held up at gunpoint (twice). It makes the job more interesting, I guess. I have my own stories.

THE PAVEMENT is beginning to shimmer when the elderly man pulls up. His forearms are shaking. He's *really* old. He hands me a sack of quarters and says it's a down payment.

"For what?" I say.

"I'm paying for the rest of my life. I figure I'll be back through twenty or thirty more times max. This should cover me."

"Sure, but," I say. "We have no way to keep track of you. How are we supposed to know it's you?"

"Well, you see my car, dontcha'?"

"What if I'm not here? There are a bunch of other lanes, see. What if someone else is in the booth?"

"You make a good point. But I *always* go through lane six. Can't you just put a note up?"

"What if you change cars or something?"

Cars behind him are honking.

"You should get an E-ZPass, sir. That's what you should do."

I hand back the sack of quarters and wave him through. But he sits there, still idling.

"Wait, don't I owe you money?"

"Forget it," I say. "This one's on me."

Twenty more times is optimistic, I think. He must be over ninety.

I GET a lot of guys in white vans. They're a regular staple. Contractors. Workers. One van pulls in, hands me the change. Four guys in back. The drivers peeks into my booth, says they could fix it up for me, make it real nice. They must be procrastinating.

"I don't own the booth, you know," I say.

"I know, but still."

"Well, what would you do?"

"Ceramic tile, maybe put a few nice light fixtures up. Stylish, you know."

I'm laughing to myself. As if I make these sorts of decisions.

"I'll get back to you," I say.

"WHAT IS your relationship with God?" the lady says. She has one of those perfect moral smiles, as if she was personally blessed by Jesus himself yesterday morning. She looks so innocent it makes you feel guilty just looking at her. As if you might stain her purity.

"It's damn good," I say. Then I think about that. "Well, good enough. I can say "damn" and he doesn't strike me down."

"Have you been saved?"

"I don't know," I say. "That's a technical question, isn't it?"

"Not particularly. It's a question of your status with the Lord."

"I'm comfortable where I am," I say. This type of conversation doesn't interest me. All speculation and theory. Nothing I can sink my teeth into.

"But you didn't answer my question."

"Thank you and have a nice day," I say. "Move along please."

"There *is* such a thing as an interventionist God, you know."

Her angelic face becomes a bit less than angelic. Everyone must suffer a fall at some point.

I DRINK half a bottle of lukewarm water. What I wouldn't give for a beer. Even a shitty wine cooler. Something. I fantasize about posting a sticky note offering customers $5 for a cold one. And it's gotta be cold.

I'd find myself jobless if I did, however. Then a guy pulls through with a case of beer in his backseat. It takes all of my willpower not to ask him for one. I mean, fuck.

Another guy pulls in and hands me his four quarters.

"Hey, is there a bathroom here, or anything?" Big fat guy with like four chins and flab under each arm. He's gotta be dying in this heat.

"Uh, no," I say. "Sorry."

"Well, where do you go when you really have to go?"

I tell him there's a building on the other side of the highway, a break room, and then he asks if he can use it. I tell him it's for employees only. What planet is this guy from?

"Well, I'm just going to have to piss right here then. Can't hold it any longer."

"Sir," I say, but he's already unzipped his fly and is pissing into an empty Big Gulp. Shit, I think. Nothing I can do at this point.

"Sir! You can't do that here. Sir!" I pick up the phone.

People are honking. Fat guy doesn't care. I wave and nod. I write down the guy's license plate number. He'll be receiving a fine from the state.

"Thank you for your time," he says. Then with one flick of his wrist, he dumps the entire Big Gulp onto the pavement in front of my booth. Speeds off.

I NEED a break. I signal this to booth one and Cheryl comes over to spell me. Thankfully, she seems to like me. Being liked has some benefits. I walk across the overpass to the central office, step inside the A/C. I have ten minutes. I close the door of the break-room behind me. I drink an entire blue Gatorade. I imagine it's something else. In the break room it's *National Esquire*, *People*, *Essence* and a few old *National Geographics*. I look through the latter. There's a pictorial from someone in Norway. Lots of ice and caribou and tall, gangly evergreens. I'd like to bottle that.

I flip through it for a few minutes and feel a bit better. Twenty more years and the house will be paid off. One day at a time, I tell myself. How else to do it? I look out the window. The air shimmers from the heat.

Exact change, I think. And how.

REST OF THE DAY I'm on autopilot. Hand out, cash. Hand out, cash. Hand out, cash. Sweating. I'm close to miserable, but I don't want to think about it. Thinking will make it that much more difficult.

I get home and shower and go see mom. They say she'll be out soon. "It's diabetes, not cancer," one of the nurses says. It's supposed to be uplifting.

Mom kisses my forehead.

"Hang in there," I say. "You'll be out soon."

"Don't *ever* get old," she says.

I know that's not the problem. I think of the guy with the bag of change.

I go home and Stouffer-it. A little ice cream sandwich makes a world of difference. Shades are drawn. Dark and chilled. I'm back tomorrow and the next day, but off the day after that.

There will be rest. I'll see Mom. Maybe throw some darts down at Jimmy's. I'll use plastic for everything—beer, wings, everything.

Next day I know I'll be back in the booth. Dreaming of Norway.

LITHING BLOOKER CRACKEN

☛

"I'M DONE," I said. "Did you hear me? Done. D. O. N. E."

It was pouring outside, rain thudding the roof so hard it was seeping into my cranium. I sat bleary-eyed in my 1998 Escort. A terrible car in every way, exterior the color of guano. Interior—snot. Mechanically the car was beyond a lemon; it was a rattling can of death.

"It's your life," he said. "When have I ever told you what you should or shouldn't do?"

"You don't seem too concerned, that's all. You weren't there. That's what I'm trying to tell you."

"So, tell me then," he said. He pulled over. We were on some unlit access road, trying to find the highway. He wouldn't admit we were lost.

I did. I told him everything Kaak-related, everything he didn't already know. I mean, yes I should never drink more than two glasses of Shiraz a night—something about it and my metabolism don't mix. And yes, I had no reason to carry on like I did with him that late without Gus present. They were friends after all. I was just along for the ride. The third wheel gf. Like that.

I wanted to talk about anything else. Gus held my hand as the other one shook.

Kaak came over wired on something, I know that for sure. What I don't know—I told Gus it was meth or speed of some brand or the other. I'm not a druggie and never have been, so I don't really know. I had told Gus before that I suspected as much about Kaak. He just had far too much energy; it wasn't just endorphins or adrenaline or high-on-life. Nobody is *that* high on life.

Still. It was fine. We were at the gazebo, watching the fireflies and talking. I was drinking Shiraz from the bottle. Kaak was going on about street smarts. He called it "Wordly Wise." "WW."

"Because I'm out there all the time just living and breathing the city I'm deeply, I mean *deeply* immersed, you know? On one plane I'm prayforming. On another—Earthly plane—I'm reading faces. I'm considering their lineage, their diet, their personal philosophies, their cosmology, their psychological profile. I see it all unscroll before my Earthly eyes while I'm simultaneously moving, moving, moving, chanting, singing, shouting, dancing. You have to: keep. Your. Eyes. Peeled. WW."

"I've heard that," I say, half meaning it.

"Ah, yes—lady of wisdom. WW, my lady. I know Senor Gus chose you for a mighty, mighty good reason."

We go on like this for a long time.

Some of it was advice. Some of it was he needed adulation (and I was seemingly available). Some of it was we rarely, if ever, had a conversation on our own away from Gus.

It was a nice summer night. The pond. The frost. The chemical uplift. The fireflies.

Kaak moved toward me inch by inch over the hours. I barely noticed—that was the thing. He was a performer. He was *physical*. He had muscles in places I didn't even know had muscles. But I realized something when I kicked my bottle and nothing came out. He knew. WW. But, loopy. He had his hands pressed into me, upstairs and downstairs. I felt the latticework against my back. He pressed into me, more than just hands. Then I was on the floor. His weight on me. A ripping. In my state I almost thought he *was* Gus or some kind of Gus amalgam. It was a blur.

When his foot hit mine, it jarred me from the moment. I looked at myself and pushed him back. He didn't register.

"We are having some moment, aren't we?"

"I need to...."

I peeled away and bolted. The grass was dewy and the frogs seemed louder. I ran through the garage door into Gus's room. I locked myself in—top and bottom. I'm glad I made him commit to both. "You never know," I said. And I was right.

I still moved the desk in front of the door. And the rolling chair. And a stack of books. I didn't know what this guy would do.

"See, I'm done," I said through the drumming rain.

Gus didn't say anything. He sat there looking at me, both hands on the wheel. Except we weren't going anywhere.

ONE THING you should know about Gus is he has a ton of money. I mean, out the wazoo. A *lot* more money than anybody else our age. To cut to the chase. Some say this was inheritance. Some say he hit it big on IPOs. I haven't a clue. But the money made him somewhat oblivious, blind to the devices of others. He didn't look the other way; he simply maintained a childlike incorruptibility.

You wouldn't guess this by looking at him—this is because he doesn't *spend* any money. He dresses like a hobo. He drives a beat-up car. He doesn't eat out or go on vacations. He basically just lives for the moment, in the moment.

But his parents gave him his *house* for a graduation present. Happy graduation! Here are the keys to a beautiful '58 house. Four bedrooms, five acres and a pool and I already mentioned the gazebo and pond. Plus, a hefty trust fund. He's set.

As a result of his "privilege," as he calls it, he tries to give back. Or at least not indulge. Gus told me once that he finds it obscene when guys with money flaunt it, making everyone around them feel worse. He wanted to steer away from that kind of statement.

"I just want to be normal and contribute in some way, do some kind of good," he told me early on.

When I met Gus he was on a Dumpster diving kick. Because he could. Because he liked the challenge. He had pared down his food expenses to twenty dollars a week—essentially food he couldn't possibly find in a Dumpster. "Twenty dollars a week should be enough for one person. Anything more than that is luxury."

Despite the money, Gus still worked. He found an office job editing the company trade journal and otherwise doing massive amounts of administrivia. He said he found the job "somewhat tedious," but that the editing component gave him something to think about. "I want to be productive. I don't want to rest on my laurels."

But after work he'd go to one of seemingly hundreds of Dumpsters he knew of and see what he could dig up. He'd take me along, though I was clearly there less because I wanted to be and more because he needed a lookout and someone to hold the bag into which he tossed his finds.

Then we'd go home to his large house and eat the spoils.

In retrospect, I'm not sure why I put up with it, but at the time he seemed so imbued with self-confidence and a kind of swagger—if swagger can be applied to fishing through the trash for food.

ONE THING neither of us knew was that there was a whole community of Dumpster divers. The second (and more important thing) neither of us knew was that once they found out Gus had a house and was a generous guy, his life would change. Of course, unlike Gus, most Dumpster divers didn't do it out of *choice* or some kind of entertainment.

For me it was a process of getting past the odors, primarily. I could handle the solids. When Gus started the venture, it was early spring and found cheese and yogurt was still basically okay. By June the stench was definitely stomach churning—the fish or moldering old meat. I would wear a lot of perfume—not my usual predilection—and think of strawberries and roses. Mostly, I was along for the ride. I was young and trying to figure out what my niche was (if I even had a niche).

The men and women Gus and I met were drunks and vets and toss-offs from the corporate world. They were once better off and were suddenly one-day-at-a-time. They slept wherever they could and lived behind an edifice of pride. They took what they could get; they lived on their wiles.

At first it was Jake and Bruce and a guy who went by Mr. X. Jake and Bruce were friends—or became so on the streets—and they did everything in tandem in a friendly and self-effacing manner. Jake owned a video store but the Netflix juggernaut put him under, and he fell into a bout of depression after he lost the store. This led to the loss of his house and marriage. Bruce was a municipal worker—parking tickets, we think—laid off and then couldn't find a thing.

"It's my own fault," he always said. "Never finished school. Can't blame Wall Street for that."

Gus invited them to crash in the basement rather than live in the shelters. After several weeks of hemming and hawing, they were there.

Then outside the city, Gus befriended Mr. X, who did parking lot murals. I liked him immediately because he gave off a warm, brotherly air—joking with me frequently and teasing me on occasion. Wide smile.

Then we came across Dougie and Grace—a couple who had to give up their daughter for adoption because they could no longer feed her. They were grieving when we met these two and Gus reached out to them, telling the couple that he was adopted and that it would all work out great for their daughter. They lived in the room right next to Gus.

Kaak was different from the others, in every way. This is the way he liked it, what he cultivated, if you ask me. His way of garnering attention perhaps. Perhaps it was affected, perhaps it wasn't.

When we first met Kaak, he was subdued. It was me, Gus, Dougie, Grace and Kaak. We were scouring a fairly large two-flap Dumpster for goodies. It was difficult work in that you had to get down *into* the Dumpster—all the way in. You couldn't just cherry-pick from the lip. Gus was a bit at odds with the Dumpster because he liked easy pickings, to hover and pull bags out and sort through them on the outside.

As the others rummaged, Kaak squatted and clenched his hands together and muttered in what I would later learn was Festadian, the language of his making. His prayer went something like this: "Lithing blook fla liy yoo tweepa! Lithing blooker cracken koop soo wee! Blooker blooken illy woo! Lithing flaythy bunto prika woo." I wondered what it meant.

And then he scrambled up the Dumpster wall and into the morass.

Afterwards I asked Kaak about his pre-Dumpster activity.

"You are such an observant soul, a wise being. You *notice* so much," he said. Kaak blinked rapidly. He had a way of doing this—I thought of it as his quasi-epileptic tic. Gus smiled at me and shrugged, as if he knew what I was thinking.

"I try," I said. Despite the obvious flattery. I couldn't help but enjoy the ten seconds of pleasure.

"Do you ever pray?" he said, his right hand gesturing an open hand to me. Was this a kind of meditation sign? Was I supposed to recognize it?

Kaak's face was receptive and smooth, a plain of gentleness I had never seen. His eyes peered into my own. It felt as if he peered into my being and rummaged inside it, searching as he just did inside the Dumpster.

"Not particularly," I said. I viewed this as two bits too intimate for an initial conversation.

"Well, perhaps we can change that?"

"Are you trying to convert me?"

He laughed and said, "Sah weedling kez fuh woo wee," and laughed some more. He knew the joke but the rest of us were lost.

"I am sorry," he said. "I am not what you would call evangelical. I am all faiths, all cultures, all peoples. I am at one with the beasts in the air and water and on land. I believe in the myth of the soul and its original creator. Beyond this...." he shrugged and smiled.

At this point I should have listened to my inner alarm, which told me: (A) This man is hiding something under his bluster and (B) His bluster forces me to view him askew (at best).

But Kaak had a way of laughing and smiling his way into one's graces. His hair pulled up into a fountain sprouting from his head in five different directions. His winking. His bow-legged walk that gave him a duck-like appearance. Yes, he was missing a few teeth and the ones remaining were crooked and mossy. And his skin was leathery and seemingly three times as thick as normal.

I did not feel threatened. I was amused.

SOON ENOUGH, Kaak was one of the others who lived in Gus's house. He and Gus would talk all night about abstractions—the role of pride or ego or wisdom in a shattered world. Oddly, they would often do this over a game of cards—usually something simple like Gin Rummy or War. Something childlike almost. They had this in common.

"You wouldn't think he's competitive, but he is," Gus said. Kaak even began teaching Gus Festadian.

"Will you accompany Gus and see one of my prayformances?" Kaak asked, suddenly. It seemed to be on a whim. It was most likely not.

"I don't know…when are they? Is this a religious thing, or something? I'm not religious."

Kaak did his laughing response thing and said at noon every day he prayformed in the park. "This is how I earn my keep." And if you made a real living, I thought, you wouldn't be mooching off some guy you met at a Dumpster dive.

"Sure, what the hey. I'll go," I said, more to escape the weirdness than anything else.

"Noon," he said.

"Yes, noon."

That night Gus slid into bed after two. I was asleep but he woke me. This immediately sent me toward a cranky state.

"Sorry," Gus whispered. "It's…"

"What gives?"

"You know, he's hard to pull away from. It just goes on and on."

"He seems like the leader of some cult, a cult of one maybe. It's strange, the whole thing."

Gus sighed and said he couldn't just toss Kaak back on the street now. Gus said he considered Kaak a kind of friend, that he had grown to like him. You can't toss a friend back onto the street.

"Do you know anything *about* him?"

"I know a lot. His lineage. His beliefs. He's a performer. I mean, look, he's interesting. Entertaining."

I felt the tug of suspicion.

"But you don't *know* him."

"What should I *know*? I don't *know* any of these people. I go on gut."

"*My* gut feeling is telling me he's way off."

"Okay. Okay."

Then we didn't say anything. Gus slept. I pretended to, I tried to, but instead I stared up at the dark ceiling for a long time. Then my eyes got tired and I did fall asleep. Thankfully.

I loved Gus. But the blindness. Also, he bored me on some deep material level.

"GENTLEMEN and ladies. Let me have your full attention," Kaak bellowed. His voice was deep and almost quavering with emotion. "My name is Kaak. K-A-A-K. In Festadian numerology this equals one one plus one plus one plus one one. *This*, sweet audience, is a sacred number, the most sacred of all. Six. The number of births, of the imagination, of the inner being. The number of sexes, of souls, of genius, of palindromes."

Then he started slowly bowing his violin, talking over it.

"I am America. I am African, Irish, Carib Indian, Romanian Gypsy, Hebrew, Russian. I am all peoples from all places. Yet, gentlemen and ladies, I am from the land of Festad, from the sixth planet from the red sun of Xalan. You may not believe this, but here I stand. I vocalize. I aerobicize. I alchemize. I act. I heal. I dance. I operate. I mythologize. I utter the language of my people. This, gentlemen and ladies, is my prayformance."

And at this Kaak bowed faster and began maniacally stomping and twirling and hooting and kicking his feet and running in place. He was a whirlwind, a thunderstorm.

I couldn't take my eyes from him. He prayformed for an hour, then vanished into the trees.

I admit it: I clapped when he came home.

"That was amazing, Kaak. Truly. Now I do see," I said. "Now I understand."

"Thank you," he said. "I am blessed with a good Qakah."

He watched my quizzical face.

"You might call it something like a violin."

"Oh, but there was so much more. I thought you were overstating it—the performance aspect. But I've never seen anyone with so much energy."

"You will make me blush," he said.

Then he said he would retire, go to sleep for a bit before dinner. He said his prayformances sapped him like nothing else.

"Yes, go rest," I said. "I will make you a nutritious meal." I would serve him.

Ninety minutes later, we ate the meal of a lifetime. Fish and a delicious fruity rice dish and bread and roasted root vegetables and chocolate and warm elixirs for his throat. I have never cooked like this before. In retrospect, it was a kind of service.

Kaak said we would now *all* eat like a Festadian king. This was his way of thanking us.

MY POSITION shifted, as positions sometimes do.

"If you would like me to teach you in the ways of prayformance, I can attempt to do so."

I could hear the frog chorus, feel the lapping wind.

"The Festad way is simple, and easy to instruct. I do not mind this role."

I sat on the porch, trying to look away from him, but at the same time finding myself magnetized.

He said the night before he stayed up until four in the morning chanting and then awoke at seven to translate a passage from English to Festadian, lest he lose his ability to do so. He said he only bathed on Sundays, adhering to the Festad tradition.

He said this balancing on his left foot.

"Do you ever attempt to rebalance yourself? It is important to practice using your non-dominant side. One cannot soar with only one wing."

"No, I have never thought of this."

His barrage seemed ceaseless.

"There is a gazebo by the pond," he said. "Perhaps we can take our little cozy chat there, join the frogs."

We walked through the dewy grass. The grass licked my ankles and the frogs croaked. The lights from Gus's house cast a white shadow on it. Kaak and I walked through the shadow and towards the gazebo. He muttered to himself in Festadian.

"Is that a prayformance, too?" I asked.

"I am a bit nervous for some reason," he said.

I didn't think of it, not at the time.

"You are?"

"I don't know," he said. "I become nervous often. It is part of the Festadian ways. WW, my darling."

When we reached the gazebo, he grabbed the lattice work, as if to keep his balance. For a moment I thought he might fall over. But the next moment I knew he wouldn't. He smiled at me. The white light hit his face just so. I could see his bicuspids gleam. And then he pressed forward into me, and then again and again.

PEANUT BRITTLE

ONE MORE rep, Wil thinks. He's been there for two hours but if he doesn't push himself he'll never even earn his own respect—and that's the low end. He knows this. One. Two. Three…Wil thrusts the shoulder press toward the whirling over-sized fans. Warehouse fans. Helicopter blades. They keep him centered, focused on the end goal. The weights clank. He looks at himself in the mirrors. Quick squeeze to his pecs when nobody's looking. Not tall—never *going* to be tall—but fucking ripped, he thinks. That's right. *Ripped*. So ripped that when people see him they are going to think, look at that muscular dude—I wonder if he is juiced. But he's not juiced. He just looks like he *could* be juiced. That's what he wants.

He struts back through the gym to the door. A group of young women loiters in the lobby in their knee high Uggs and yoga pants and shoulder-length hair. A throng of fuzzy-footed storm troopers.

Wil drives home.

Kelley is waiting for him. He knows he's late and that tonight is his turn to make dinner. Thankfully, he has those frozen Indian TV dinner thingies.

"Hey, Kel," Wil says, flinging his coat over the bannister. "I love you. Glad to be home."

"Hey," she says. "Are we eating tonight?"

"I'm so freaking jacked still," he says and scoops her up and lifts her over his shoulders. She wriggles and laughs and he lifts her again. One, two, three. He may be short but he doesn't have to be scrawny. They called him "shrimpy" when he was a kid. He'll never be shrimpy again. Never again overlooked. He's shiny and bald save for a thin crescent of hair. It looks like an apostrophe. But he's ripped, who are *they*?

It's already eight-thirty six. How did he spend so much time at the gym? Time just melts away at the gym. At the gym everything is right. At the gym he is just himself. He doesn't have to think about anyone else. Other people don't even exist. It's perfect.

"Oh, God. I'm sorry, Kel. I had to take a work call and it just went on and on," he lies. Better to lie than address the yawning rhinoceros frothing in the corner.

She shrugs. "So, what are we eating?" It's Wednesday. His day.

He snaps the freezer door open. "Punjabi kadhi and palak paneer. Which one do you want?

"Um, I *cooked* last night."

"But these are good."

It's not really cooking, she says. It's *heating*.

What's the difference? It tastes good. I'm preparing something that tastes good.

"But we agreed."

Kel leans into her laptop. Wil can tell she's disappointed. She *should* be. He *is* a disappointment. Deep down—on some elemental level—he knows this.

This is nothing new. He hates himself ten times more than she could ever hate him. And she doesn't hate him, she just finds him uninspiring and lackluster. Unless he can put together a decent meal, which is a rarity. Unless he takes her out to a decent meal, which is more likely.

She deserves better. The other day, Kelley made him homemade pasta with scallops and homemade marinara and a delicious arugula salad with fresh tomatoes and endive and shaved cucumber and homemade honey mustard dressing. He can still taste those scallops in the back of his mind—perfectly sautéed.

"Wait until Friday," Wil says. "I'm going to knock your socks off. The gym set me back tonight, my bad."

Yeah, big talker. Next time don't promise anything, moron. She's disappointed because he mentioned Thai curry and roasted pears.

She rolls her eyes back into her screen. For her part, Kelley is cute but not hot exactly. She is taller than Wil and leggy and classically beautiful. But he finds her physically dull and predictable. She has an interesting face—a nose that slightly turns to the left, lips that are just a touch asymmetrical and her neck always seems somewhat too long for her torso—out of proportion somehow. But to Wil she's like the Olive Garden of girlfriends—she won't make you gag, but she's *unexciting*. Perhaps Wil has just been with Kelley for too long, too many rounds. Stale bread.

Wil rips the cardboard packaging. One for him, one for her. He slips them into the microwave sheepishly and steps out onto the concrete slab patio. Smokes a furtive cigarette. All that hard work in the weight room nullified. His stress level is right back where it was after work. Wil subverts his own progress regularly.

He smells of b.o. and gym funk, which combines with the odors from the frozen Indian into a powerfully pungent gaseous swirl.

He watches the glass microwave plate circle. Two plastic cups of tepid water. Forks. Napkins. The cups read: "You are Klassy!" Some Saturday morale booster work thing from five, six years ago.

Wil doesn't notice any lingering resentment in Kelley as they eat. "Not bad, right?"

She chews and nods. She's good at masking and repressing though, Wil knows. Her eyes are still on the laptop screen. This is their third iteration as a couple and if they don't know each other's bullshit by now, they never will. No illusions though: they agreed this time that if it doesn't work out, that's it. No more emotional gymnastics. It's get married or never speak to each other again— nothing in the middle.

Kelley still has her apartment, though, and the dresser is half empty. Either way, Wil's shitty two-bedroom condo is not a long-term solution.

After dinner, Wil wipes the plates with a paper towel and slides them into the dishwasher.

"Sorry if the meal seems half-assed, Kel. I'll do better. It was the gym."

Kel shrugs. "Are we still on *this*?" She sounds more weary than annoyed.

Her sense of resignation is not lost on him. Still, she is sweet and doting in her own way, when she can be. He considers himself lucky, at least on some basic level.

They read magazines in bed and watch the hockey game. Wil isn't counting but it's been at least two sexless weeks in a row. He is forty-four though: he should be good to himself. He shouldn't expect much and should just be content. Meditate more. Drink more herbal tea. They sleep with a nightlight on in the corner outlet. It washes out the shadows, basks the corner in a nostalgic glow. There is nothing childish about this.

WIL'S COMMUTE is a manageable thirty-two minutes plus or minus. He read somewhere that thirty-five minutes is now the nationwide average and some experts postulate that the half hour commute acts as a healthy buffer between two worlds, an emotional transition. So he's three minutes away from ideal. He's doing so great. He takes another glance at himself in the rearview.

Wil imagines small town Midwestern pharmacists must think East Coasters are insane and in deep denial.

During the drive to work Wil listens to hard edge industrial music, mostly. He grew up with Nine Inch Nails and Nitzer Ebb and progressed (or regressed) from there. Skinny Puppy, Die Krupps, Icon of Coil. Plenty of obscure Scandinavian and German acts. He tries to ignore the quasi-Nazi vibe of this music and just feel the energy. His eardrums pulse and he slams the dashboard and steering column along to the pounding beat as he navigates the stop and go traffic. Sunglasses. Ten-year-old Acura. Snacking on pop tarts and now-cold, oily coffee at the longer lights.

At work, Wil tries to find a way to amuse himself. Technically a "programmer," Wil mostly manages a series of gaming websites for a company in England. Jolly Games. He hates computer games himself and always has, which cuts into his motivation. The websites are so well programmed these days they all but manage themselves. The company is replete with cash and Wil has little to do with his time. Mostly, he plays solitaire and checks his Facebook feed. He knows more about the lives of his high school buddies now than he did when he was in high school.

Recently, however, Wil has found himself gravitating more and more to Margie Thatch. Several weeks prior, Wil was looking for a book or DVD on Margaret Thatcher—as a gift for Wil's uncle who lived in England for years during the Thatcher era—and found her equally obnoxious and fascinating. Instead, he stumbled across Margie's page. Thatch, not Thatcher. Nineteen and a student at a college in Indiana (Lakewood College, it seems) her pictures were flirtatious but not slutty, becoming but not voluptuous. They struck the right balance for Wil. And, unlike so many other women his age on Facebook, she wasn't content to only post pictures of her children or various exotic places she's traveled to. Or her fucking pets in adorable fucking positions. Margie seemed both intelligent and down-to-Earth and accessible, he could tell. He thinks of himself as a keen observer of the human condition. He thinks of himself as a step ahead of everyone else.

In his cubicle Wil stares at Margie again, refreshing his browser every five minutes to see if she updates her Facebook profile pic. Wil clicks on her (many) publically available photos—but that is not enough access. Wil desperately wants to "friend" her, to see the photos only her friends could see—the more revealing ones perhaps—but he doesn't dare. He can't bring himself to. Never—even though his cursor frequently floats over the "friend" button. One click. That's all it will take—one click. At any rate, she would never accept his friendship, he knows deep down. She was a college student at a seemingly Christian college in Indiana, with her college friends and her pert body and perfect face and smile. His short old bald head and saggy skin would do nothing for her. You can't advertise experience. She'd call the police or his boss or contact Kelley or the IRS or FBI or she'd give him a computer virus somehow. Reasonable fears. It was impossible. She would see him as a creepy old guy with a mid-life crisis. Slimy palms.

Shame washes over Wil and he minimizes Facebook and returns to monitoring the websites that don't need monitoring and then back to solitaire for an hour, until it is time to eat. He read somewhere that Germans laugh at Americans and their lack of productivity (their addiction to disposable entertainment). Makes sense.

At the restaurant across the street, he stuffs his face with the Grand Texan burger, curly fries and a tall Pepsi. A large meal for lunch for him. Wil eats alone, his smart phone keeping him company in the corner. Above him, a framed print of hunting dogs chasing foxes across a grassy knoll as the huntsmen shout and lift bugles to their perfect lips.

On his napkin Wil writes, "I need...." But he can't complete the sentence. He isn't sure what he's trying to say, even to himself.

SIX MONTHS AGO, they settled on the "arrangement." Kelley would stay at his place four days a week—Monday through Thursday and the weekends would be ad hoc, mostly utilizing her apartment closer to the city as their base. This way, Kelley argued, they would have enough togetherness to justify a relationship, but enough potential for solitude to stay sane, especially if Monday through Thursday were downbeat or less than expected.

As a Thursday, this put all the pressure on Wil. No gym. And the dinner must dazzle or the subpar performance would linger all the way until Monday. Wil arrives home at five-thirty since he ducked out half an hour early—claiming stomach indigestion (which was partially true, as a result of the beef patties piled up in his small intestines). He has a good ninety minutes before Kelley would be home—plenty of time to figure out something nice. The fridge is stocked, or stocked enough to appease a foodie. And he is a short guy—he doesn't need that much to eat—this is mostly a kind of offering to her. A blessing.

But instead of researching recipes and making dinner preparations, Wil sits in front of the computer, scrolling through Margie Thatch's pictures, saving the JPGs and enlarging the pics to full screen so he could examine the beauty that is Margie. He knows he'll eventually *have* to contact her. He won't be able to live with himself otherwise. He could forgive himself his creeper/stalker tendencies later. Wil likes to think of himself as courageous despite his physical limitations (or perhaps because of them). He certainly is not afraid of rejection—or at least he doesn't *think* he is.

That said, he has to wait for the right time. Intuitively, he feels that it might be when his standing with Kelley rests on more confident ground. He'll emanate self-assurance as a result of a greater sense of appreciation and standing in the world.

While he has Margie's pictures up on the screen, Wil researches, to the best of his ability, given privacy restrictions, her love life and various friendships. This is tough since they aren't friends, but he is still able to access enough recent images to tell that she appears to be mostly single. The majority of her pictures feature her along with her pretty (but not *as* pretty) lady friends. No suck-face pictures with Jimmy or Bobby or Cal. No romantic walks along the beach. And the profile pic is her in a cute-but-not-overtly-sexy baby-blue sun dress kicking back her heals against a sunny orange background. She might be open to, at least, flirting online with him, perhaps. Getting to know him. He's a *nice* guy. He's just a guy in great shape who wants to get to know her a bit better. What's the harm?

When Wil looks at his watch it is already 6:30.

Crap! He has to get himself going. He looks up a quick recipe for lasagna, which is usually a winner. Even though he doesn't have ricotta, he can substitute cottage cheese (plucking out the mushy pineapple chunks) and despite the lack of tomato sauce, he might be able to get by with diluted tomato paste. He could just spread it thin, make it a schmear of sorts. And though he is out of good wine he does have an old bottle of mostly flat champagne that he can mix with Sprite or seltzer. A little cheap mixed-drink of sorts. And though he doesn't have any fresh bread or lettuce on hand he can chop up some carrots and put out the pasty hummus from last week. She will probably just be happy he made the effort. He hopes.

Wil has to wonder if he isn't, on some level, sabotaging again. Perhaps, deep down, he doesn't *really* want it to work out with Kelley at all. Perhaps he wanted an excuse to pursue other newly found options.

While preparing the meal, he overcooks the noodles (distracted by more pics of Margie on his smart phone) and mishandles the noodles anyway—they break and are otherwise mangled and gummy. The filling seems functional—ground turkey and diced green peppers and onions, but with the pineapple cottage cheese (he forgot to pluck the pineapple—more online pics) and schmear tomato paste Wil can tell the lasagna will be dry and an overall catastrophe. He kicks himself for taking the ingredients for granted earlier.

Luckily, Kelley is running a bit late (had to stop at the CVC, renew her prescriptions), which gives Wil enough time to have the casserole in the oven before she opens the door. Once she arrives, he quickly makes a decent salad and fruit salad, hoping to distract Kelley from the piss-poor casserole attempt with the heavy-handed salad overkill—six or seven different veggies in addition to the lettuce in one and a thousand colors in the fruit salad (let the rainbow affect blind her). While Kelley changes, he mixes the flat champagne with the Sprite and to his taste buds it's not exactly *dreadful*.

KELLEY TAKES it all in—the dueling salads, the odd cottage cheese, pineapple and tomato paste concoction, the flat champagne distilled with soda ("ghetto mimosa," she called it later).

But she doesn't say a thing at first. She eats.

It was only after trying everything—about five minutes in—that she fully understands the symbolism.

"We're over, aren't we?"

"What?" Wil takes a bit of the nearly inedible lasagna. He scoops the filling out and leaves the gummy noodles to disintegrate on the far edge of his plate.

"Is *this* your best effort?"

"I'm trying," he says. "I'm tryyyying here."

"Yeah," she said. "I can see the *attempt*."

FRIDAYS ARE Wil's favorite day of the week (another quality that makes him original, he thinks; most working slobs love Saturdays or Sundays)—the casual dress, the early dismissal. "Dismissal"—nothing like that word to emasculate him (in his mind all he can think about is middle school).

But even better: Wil doesn't have Kelley on Fridays—unless they expressly make plans. He is home-free. And he didn't. He didn't want to or need to. Theirs is a relationship he often wants a vacation from. No, this Friday is time for Wil to hunker down with Margie's page. A little Throbbing Gristle on the speakers and a cold beer—perfect. Later, takeout pizza with sausage and olives—even later (if he felt like it), back to the gym.

Maybe this will be the night he'd friend her?

After a couple beers and a tug Wil feels sufficiently relaxed enough. At first his cursor hovers ever-so-delicately over the "add friend" button. Then. He clicks it. He walks to the fridge for another beer, but before he can even return to the computer, he hears the pinging Facebook notification. She accepts his friendship.

She is a friend collector. One of those. For once, this works in his favor. Usually, it added up to nothing but additional aggravation and duty—more painful parties to attend, more favors to grant.

Wil is giddy with excitement, so much so he doesn't even know where to start. Should he ogle the many more photos he now has access to? Should he send her a pm declaring his love for her and making wild proclamations about her beauty and their future together? Should he post something funny and jokey on her wall to alleviate any stress (his or hers)? It is utterly overwhelming actually. He glances through a few images, but when his hand starts shaking with excitement, he knows it is time to go to the gym. After all, he will need to impress this young lady with his brute physicality. He wants muscles on top of muscles for the pic he would send her.

The dude at the counter stops Wil as he attempts to check in with his I.D.

"Wait a minute. Wil. With one 'l'? What is that about, if you don't mind me asking?"

"I don't know," Wil says. "My parents were trying to be minimalists or something. Maybe I only have half a normal will? I think it might be Welch or something. Who knows?"

"That's funny," the dude says.

"Not if you're me. They used to call me 'Peanut.' You think that's better?"

"That's funny, too. Wil with one L. Huh."

"Like I said. I like it."

"Yeah, me too. Unique."

The dude smirks and scans Wil through. Wil knows the dude does *not*, in fact, like it. He's just paid to say nice things but secretly he's laughing to himself.

"Have a good one."

Wil surprises himself by flashing a peace sign—even though it is a deeply sarcastic peace sign.

During his workout Wil takes a peek at his phone just to double-check (despite the "no phone rules"). Yes, she is still his friend. This can be something, he thinks. It just might. Wil tries to tamp down his erection. To accomplish this, he thinks of Kelley barking at him for the lame lasagna. It works!

He goes back to squats and bench presses and shoulder presses and curls. He can look at himself in the mirror and focus on his goals, his wants, his desires. He isn't exactly a gym rat, not as regular as some of the guys (and he doesn't care a whit about meeting workout buddies), but he is regular enough. And he doesn't even need a work-out buddy.

"I'M JUST a guy," Wil writes. "But I have eyes. I can tell you with all honesty, you are the most beautiful woman I've ever seen. That is all. I have no realistic aims or goals here. Or illusions. I like your mug."

He sends the pm.

After half an hour, no response. Still friends.

After two hours, no response. Still friends.

Wil can see that she had read the message.

The next morning he types: "I see that you received my message. Forgive me, please, if came across too strong. Too forceful. It's just that you are very, very pretty. I'm sure you know this. Feel free to let me know what kind of music you listen to. I prefer industrial. I'll make you a mix cd, if you'd like. Do people still do that? Also, I'm pretty ripped, as you can see." It all sounds absurd and infantile. Also pathetic.

He doesn't care. He sends the pm anyway. As soon as he clicks "send" he knows he made the wrong decision.

No response.

No response.

Nothing.

No.

During the early afternoon Kelley calls (probably to see how Wil is doing—a normal, considerate thing to do). Wil sees her number pop up and doesn't answer the phone.

No response from Margie still. Nothing. Still friends.

By the end of the day. Still friends.

Kelley calls again, but Wil ignores it.

The next morning: nothing from Margie. Wil writes again. "I've been looking at your page and am I crazy or do you enjoy the music of Drake and Charlie Mars and Frank Ocean. I don't know them, but I'm intrigued by your musical tastes. I'm brushing up on your interests and I hope to be familiar with their tunes by the next time we chat. That way it's not just about me. I want to learn about you as well. We can learn about each other, slowly. We will have a common interest. A platform for further discussion."

After an hour, no response. Message read. Still friends.

After two hours, same thing.

After three hours, not friends. No access to her pics or to Margie Thatch at all. Blocked. He does find a Margaret Thatcher Fan page in looking for Margie Thatch. Seven hundred thousand and change fans. He joins just for the sake of proximity. Just the ex-prime minister's name has Wil thinking of the other one. The one he wants to think about.

ON MONDAY MORNING Wil calls Kelley from the car (he just then realizes he hasn't talked to her all weekend). He even turns down the music. But she doesn't pick up. He leaves a message: "Hey, Kel. Just wondering what we're having for dinner tonight. I think it's you tonight. Um, I'll be home by around six. Give me a call if you need anything from the store. Happy to get them for you."

But Kelley doesn't call back and doesn't respond to his texts or e-mails.

Nothing.

He should have called her back over the weekend. He knows this. That would have been considerate.

On his phone, Wil looks at the picture of Kelley standing in front of the fountain at the faux town center. She wears yoga pants and knee high boots and so did the friends she stands next to, right leg kicked up jauntily. What strikes Wil is the fact that they all look the same—beautiful hair, too much makeup, white teeth and then the latest fashionable uniform. She was one of many women just like her (Margie seems different, extraordinary). Is this sameness what guys like or what women think guys like or both? Or neither? Is it some kind of corporate glaze?

That night Wil eats chicken with mixed vegetables from the Chinese takeout place down the street. He opens a fake Facebook page under the obviously fake name Peanut Brittle and he searches for Margie Thatch. But nothing comes up. Wil blames the Facebook algorithms. He'd have to be patient, he knows. He'd have to friend some people at Lakewood College and then he'd be friends with her friends and he'd be able to see his love. But even this didn't work. Wil contemplates the worst-case scenario: she deleted her Facebook account entirely or made the privacy settings so extreme that nobody but her intimates could gain access to her photos (only one or two bad pics were on Google proper, and these were from the time she was on her high school soccer team).

Peanut Brittle—that describes him perfectly, he realizes. All his life he was destined to become Peanut Brittle. A brittle little turd of a legume. And even more so since he doesn't eat peanuts. He's allergic to himself. He's a stupid, needless sweet. An afterthought.

For now, those few pics would have to do, Wil realizes. Better than nothing. He'd figure this puzzle out, he tells himself, if it takes him all year. He has tons of time now that Kelley is seemingly on the outs, again. Who cares? And next time—no friending Margie. Nothing will mess it up. It will be a precious little fragile egg of a relationship and he'll be the idiot with the nest of mothballs protecting it. No monkey business. He has staring to do and nothing will frighten her away from that.

I AM NOT A HAMSTER!

FROM UP on the corner StairMaster, I can see everything. Everything that matters, anyway—the muscle hombres, the brittle old ladies walking gingerly on the treadmills, the gangly college kids avoiding stats study group, the power yoga class in full swing, Mr. Stretchy on the mats, the adrenaline biking class in back—music thumping loud.

Me, I like the StairMaster. I feel like I *am* getting somewhere, climbing to the top of the Empire State Building, scaling Mount Whitney. I know I'm not, but I can imagine it.

Diamond Gym likes the exclamation mark! I have come to embrace it myself! With the exclamation mark life seems so much more exciting! It makes me feel less down-spirited and sour about my current state of employment (which is no employment)! And lack of a love life!

Twenty minutes of StairMaster on seven or eight and I'm a sweaty hog. I wipe everything down with the humdrum antiseptic spray (is it just water?) and paper towel combo—though after I douse sweat on the StairMaster they should just blow it up and build another one. The guy who works out with rubber gloves—I understand that guy. I sit there with my sweaty self on the little stiff plastic bench next to the water fountain, leaning over for a drink every other minute, my sweat adhering my ass to the stiff little bench.

I'm right below STRENGTHEN! Diamond is big into slogans. On the other wall—above the free weights—is ENDURE! HEALTHY! Is above the Nautilus machines and FITNESS! Is above the entrance/exit in case you forget why you came here or what the purpose was. They'll remind you!

I get a second wind somehow after all that Empire State Building climbing. I'm ready for more, only this time at a slower pace.

He's sprinting up the stairs and has been since I slumped my flabby ass into DG. And he's barely sweating. He looks actually bored. Little Gnome Guy is churning his little gnome legs next to me. StairMaster on seventeen! Nobody else but him could come anywhere close to pulling that off.

I'm on three, slowing trudging upwards next to him, embarrassed. Gnome Guy glances at my reading, smirks, directs his attention straight ahead. This is the usual stare-straight-ahead-so-as-to-avoid-the-necessity-of-talking-or-smiling-or-making-eye-contact-with-the-other-DG-drones look. We've all seen it before.

I am not a hamster! I think. First of all, hamsters never move this sluggishly. But also: hamsters don't think about career planning and the irony that is the gaggle of muscle hombres at two o'clock (they strive to be individuals rooster-thrusting their muscular torsos, but they all look the same, dress the same, same ear-buds-and-I-pod-strapped-to-their-bicep look). Like something from *Running Man* or some other bad "futuristic" 80's film. I'm averting my eyes from Gnome Guy (ashamed) and watching the various news shows blare on the big flat screens positioned up in the sky every six inches. I have three more months of checks coming and after that I'm into savings. Emily is already frustrated at me. *For* me, also. Because she's supportive, or pretends to be for my benefit. But also, partially *at* least, at me—though she would never admit it. She is too kind and considerate to verbalize frustrations (I am not). I'm sure I'll get an interview next week. Or the week after. PCI is right up my alley, and the headhunters are out there hunting heads. They have a vested interest.

Gnome guy ups the ante to eighteen. He's unbelievable. His little legs are churning like crazy, and yet it's almost as if he's weightless. His feet lightly pad each step. He's a freak of nature (in a good way).

I want to ask him really badly—a) for how long do you work out?, b) how do you *do* it?, c) what is your purpose in life?

Impressive.

But I can't. I don't want to ruin the guy's groove and plus maybe he's ruminating about Proust or Hegel or something or turning his latest invention over and over in his mind. He looks intelligent—maybe even genius-level (though it's always hard to tell).

This is when I realize the true purpose of the various televisions—all set to different channels—is to lasso the eyes of the "clients" and distract them long enough that they (we) don't think to speak to each other and ask basic questions as to what the fuck? The screens are there to smooth over the innate aggression, to pacify.

For the majority (especially for those who work) this may have a sedating effect. As someone who goes to the gym twice a week as something to pass the time, I could go without.

I used to go to the basement of the Y to lift weights when I was sixteen. This is different.

I see old stretchy on the rowing machine, pulling back and stretching his gazelle neck to the left, then pulling back and stretching his neck to the right.

The housewives are going into the ENDURE! Studio for Ab Fab—the crunch class. Yoga pants rule there, also. Some Katy Perryesque number gyrates from the two dozen speakers. Every song at DG sounds the same, as if generated by an army of pink and lime green robots. It's upbeat! It's "fun"!

A trainer with Trainer! Plastered across his standard black and orange t-shirt bends over a fat man and a medicine ball (in vogue again, I've noticed).

Towel guy carefully places his towel on the quad lift Nautilus machine. Everybody, of course, checks everybody else out—either directly or via mirror.

Little gnome continues his churning. He's a machine.

"Still going at it?" I actually say. I don't plan on saying it; I blurt. He has ear buds.

He sees my mouth move or my stupid smile.

He plucks a bud out.

"What's that?"

"Nothing. I just said 'still going at it?'"

At this juncture he could a) be the kind of gnome who clamps his ear bud back on and ignores me, b) say "What does it look like?" pissed that I interrupted his "flow" or c) talk between puffs.

"Yeah, good workout," he says, like the churning automaton he is.

He is not even breathing hard.

While I have his attention, I decide why not?

"How do you do it? It's *amazing*."

"Do what?"

"You're going so fast and you aren't even tired."

He explains that he does marathons and started when he was in college and just kept on doing it. This is just a snack for him, he says. A way for him to keep "somewhat in shape." I'd hate to see a full meal.

"How long do you usually stay here?"

"Maybe three or four hours. You just get used to it. This is my normal."

He's so utterly nice and pleasant and down-to-Earth. But I simply cannot let him beat me. I decide then and there that my goal for the day is to outlast him—to see Gnome Guy walk out the door with me still inside, sweating it out.

"Nice talking to you," I say and shut down the StairMaster.

I wipe off, get another drink and sit for a spell. I'm watching

Gnome Guy the entire time. He's still going at it. When I go to DG I usually do the StairMaster, some light stretching over on the bars and if I'm feeling ambitious maybe a few minutes on the rowing machine for shits and giggles.

I have some serious time to occupy in the gym if I'm going to outlast Gnome Guy.

I head over to the mats, which strike me as the most unsanitary segment of DG—all those sweaty asses stretching there. I wipe off the mat with extra vigor before doing anything (maybe I'm turning into Towel Guy?).

I do sit ups.

I do little calf stretches.

I do the bridge. I do a few pushups (seven) until I'm tired.

I'm watching two young ladies—maybe college students. They have incredible bodies, though I'm not particularly attracted to their faces. They are both contorted (on separate mats) in strange positions, chatting about last weekend.

Two mats over, a gangly middle-aged woman is doing, by-the-looks-of-it, lower back stuff. Stretchy flexibility stuff.

Gnome Guy is still going at it on the StairMaster.

Another (faster) Katy Perryesque song thumps through the speakers. Auto-tune over computer dinkydinkdinks.

I'm thinking about Emily at work, moving her legs around under the desk, pinned there. I feel at once guilty and grateful to be here, moving my body. Our fight the week before last was the tip of the iceberg, I know. She said if I feel worthless, I can always get a part-time job. I'm paralyzed though, too-ashamed to stoop to the level of barista. Maybe it's a guy thing.

I hit the bathroom, pass by the muscle crew and the McLaughlin Group trying to solve the world's problems on the rickety stationary bikes. They're fixated on Bernie, pro and con—watching Fox News as they pontificate.

I ride the stationary bike next to them for a while, watching soccer and my Calories-burned count. Twenty minutes—not too bad. I turn around and Gnome Guy is still running full-steam ahead.

I do ten minutes on the rowing machine. Old Stretchy is thankfully sayonara—he makes me feel antiquated just watching him. It's late enough in the afternoon that people are starting to come in wearing their work clothes, gym bag slung over their shoulders.

I'm tired. My muscles ache. I'm sweaty as hell. I'm weary of the fakey-fake thumping music. I go back to the mats, lie down on my back (damn the germs). At first, I do some calf/Achilles stretches, then I just lie there without doing a thing at all. I drift off, Katy Perry's auto-tune minions ribboning through my head.

"Hey," I feel something or someone on my shoulder. "Hey." Again. I open my eyes and see one of the trainers crouching next to me. His nametag reads "ED!"

"You okay?"

"Yeah, just a little tired," I say.

When I lift my neck, I notice the light has dimmed through the front windows. I look at my watch—6:00. Emily will either laugh at me or think I'm making it up.

I need to find a damn job. I'll try again tonight, I will. I feel energized.

I look back at the StairMaster, but Gnome Guy is nowhere to be seen. I scan around the gym and I don't see him anywhere. In a way I won, but not in the way I would have wanted to (and not retaining consciousness—not sure sleeping counts). Healthy! Fitness!

Strengthen! Endure!

I lift myself to my feet. The trainer helps me.

"Take care now. Hope you feel better. If you need a session with me, let one of my associates up front know. I'm sure they could pop you right into my schedule."

"Thank you," I say. Groggy.

The cleaning crew is out. The vacuum guy has a strap-on vacuum cleaner going. He doesn't see it, but I give him the thumbs up.

I wonder how many calories Gnome Guy burnt today. 2,000?

It doesn't matter, I think. It's not really a competition. Only in my head.

RULE THE DAY

"HIT ME with the cheesy poofs, will ya?" Candi can be insistent and brow-archy when I'm on a Demon Warrior roll. I punt the barrel her way, fending off a cross-bow barrage, whilst eviscerating an ogre with the scimitar I got off a dusty hobgoblin whore named Ulla. The ogre's intestines uncoil onto the mud and he collapses backward. I kick his intestines at his head.

"Booyah!"

"It's two-twenty," Candi says, orange flecks on her lips. She's slurping a Yoo-Hoo. I should call Gretchen, but she thinks I won't be home from Philly until tomorrow p.m. She was first, anyway. Candi doesn't enjoy feeling like leftovers. They both know, but don't want to know. Knowing but not knowing is the worst kind of knowing. As Willow says, "just because you're poly doesn't mean you're not human." Willow is third.

I'm skulking through the soupy Poisonwood Forest, peripherals googly from eyeing the shadows for swamp chimeras and winged trolls.

Candi yawns.

"Can we sack out soon? I'm toast."

I keep trudging. Chain mail a-clacking.

"In a few."

But two ogre onslaughts and a freshly slaughtered goblin prince later and she's out cold, hand deep within the belly of the cheesy poof barrel. Feeling a twinge of something reminiscent of guilt, I pause the onslaught and put the system to sleep. Three-thirty nine is a decent time to call it anyway. Average.

Candi isn't exactly light—she's hippy and thick from the waist down (though slender and Elfish upstairs). But I manage. And by three-forty six we're snoozing to the twinkly wind chimes my father bought me from one of his Ashram-oriented sojourns. "Quests," he calls them. Whatevs.

By four-eleven, the world goes fuzzy.

I'm not in a hurry.

It isn't the lawn mower. It's not the parade of dog walkers up and down the sidewalk. It's not the roofers over at the Orenhauser's or the stream of tangerine light hemorrhaging through the gash between the double-ply curtains. What wakes me is the smell of basic coffee coupled with female voices downstairs straining to keep it to a murmur for my sake.

My life is hackneyed.

I just realize I neglected to turn on the oscillating fan last night. Now I'm paying for it.

Two-sixteen p.m.

I can tell before I even open the door it's going to be one of those cringe-y days.

Gretchen's throaty voice is intertwining with Candi's quasi-squeak like some kind of estrogen-y DNA staircase—all bad news for me. Gretchen is out of the dark, I'm thinking as I tuck my junk back into the mouth of my plaid boxers my father purchased on a find-your-genetic heritage tour to Scotland he took two summers ago—he's only a quarter Scottish, so I'm not sure which part of himself he was trying to find. Gretchen should still be "understanding"—on paper at least. We're all open polies, as opposed to those polies-for-life chumps. The latter might as well not even be polies at all as far as I'm concerned.

"Oh, hey—look who it is," squawks Gretchen. I can smell her menthol breath from here. But now she expects a kiss anyway. I do the bare minimum, then scratch for coffee.

"So?"

"So," she says.

"Oh, hey—how was Philly?"

I'm sifting a heap of that non-dairy creamer crap into my smudged blue mug.

"Not bad," I sniff.

"Oh, good-good-good," Gretchen says. "Cause, you know, Candace here was telling me the two of you chilled out, you know. Played some games and shit. Smoked some. You know."

I sniff and tell myself to play it like a duck.

"It was a *virtual* tour of Philly," I say, spooning my joe. "I went up here." I'm tapping my head, but not too hard. It's early.

"Ohhhh, I see," Gretchen says. "I'll keep that in mind." She makes that face she makes, all disapproving and high-horsey.

"It's early," I say.

"You know, the sun goes *down* in a few hours."

"Let's just go downstairs," Candi says, with an upbeat cadence. "Why don't we?" Always trying to play peacemaker.

Gretchen shoots eye daggers my way. I shrug.

I'm lurking behind my coffee mug. I pour myself a bowl of Count Chocula, tell them I'll be right down.

My Trolls and Elves calendar says I have sword fighting at five thirty, kickball at seven thirty (indoor practice). Tomorrow is going to be the beast though—supposed to visit Grandma's headstone with Shelley. Crap, I think. I should call Shelly. I shouldshouldshould. Let's not look too far ahead. I shovel back to my bowl of bobbing brown and go back down where I belong. Squabbling girlfriends await. Hopefully mediated by more Demon Warrior. If not, fuck it.

As I pad down to the man den, I know Gretchen has calmed down. I can already smell her smoking menthols out in the yard. She'll come back sated and ready to let me tackle her and pin her arms down. She digs that. If only I had a mutt it would be a perfect boring family.

"Should" is my true demon.

TO ANSWER the obvious question, no my mother doesn't approve. Father is too busy finding his bliss, traveling the world. My brother avoids me. This is what happens when a family explodes as a result of an affair and a quick exit (father's "doings").

My thing is this: I need to carve out enough space so that I can explore Wesley Abraham Ivey. One life to live and all that. I used to find myself easily pinned-down by various "obligations" and "duties," but then I realized that these are simply manifestations of my own view of how the world *should* behave. It doesn't *have* to be that way.

This evening I'm at the dojo, slicing the air with my thirty-six inch band of steel. I'm drilling, mostly "working patterns as well as muscles," is what Anne the Instructor says (if only she were poly, my life would be complete—not that I haven't attempted). Greed is the root of all evil.

Then she sets me up with Damien for sparring. Damien is a six foot seven Ichabod Crane type. Moves in a cloddy deliberate way. Facial expression makes him look as if he is constantly suffering from constipation. We spar and I have the clear upper-hand through most of it, though I somehow lose my concentration watching Damien clomp toward me with his canoe feet. I end up pinning him and getting my "poke" for a W. Good work-out, good outlet.

Kickball is less Zen-like, less cardio. More about finding the next fuck-buddy—for most of the team, at least. We spend more time talking about what we did last weekend than actually kicking the ball and running around the bases. Sure, there's Gina, who one of those mousey know-it-all types. Then there's James who is just on another planet. Elvin is obscured by his ignorance of the human condition. Most are good, solid American types.

I'm there with the team and we're snacking on animal crackers (I'm snapping the legs off with my teeth and making braying zebra noises).

Jenna is talking about a bar called the Fishin' Hole, where she got tanked and started molesting the life-sized plastic cowboy. The team sniggers at her, but she tells the story in such utter self-mockery (and need for attention?) that it's almost painful. I bite off the animal heads next.

One Gloomy Gus named Phil mutters: "What the hell am I doing with my life?" He squirrels his eyebrows. But the rest of the team tells him to chillax.

"We're here to have fun," Aimee says, pulling at her tank top strap. C'mon.

He doesn't say a thing after that.

Someone kicks the ball, which goes straight up and hits one of the gym ceiling beams. Automatic out. We all laugh.

Gloomy Gus stares straight ahead.

WHEN I GET HOME from the Fishin' Hole, I call Shelley. She only lives five blocks away, but with this many beers in my gut I'd rather just let my phone bill work for me. Talking with my mother in person can push me in all the wrong directions.

"I'm not going to be able to make it tomorrow," I say.

Silence. I can hear her shuffling some papers. Then a quick, annoyed little sniff. Hate those.

"That's okay," she says. Then more silence. She's waiting to hear my reasoning.

"I'm not feeling so great," I say. "Allergies."

My excuse is rote, but fairly waterproof. She cannot *prove* I don't feel better than I say I do (I do tend to overuse this one, however).

"Well, you'll be missed," she says. "Your grandmother was sure a special person."

"Yes. She was. She certainly was."

I think of her last year, how she sat crumpled in her favorite recliner, afghan over her waist. She wasn't a talker or a complainer, but she would grit her teeth; I can only imagine the pain she was in.

"So what did you do today?" This is a trap: seemingly an innocent question, but designed to lure me into revealing that I don't feel as badly as I say I do.

"Oh, you know—my usual. But I'm in a fog from all the allergy medication. So....I cut back, Shelley."

"What are you taking?"

I tell her I can't remember the name of the drug.

"I always seal myself inside, close the windows and all that."

"That's sage advice," I say. "You go on ahead tomorrow. I'll join you another time."

She tries to reschedule with me, but I'm not falling for that one."

"I need to go lie down now," I say. "I'm a bit cloudy."

"You mean tipsy."

I sniff. I wander off muttering.

THE PROBLEM WITH living in a small town is that nobody ever leaves said small town. My family is large enough to create the frequent pressure of engagement.

I know Shelley— first among others—considers me juvenile, a kind of man-boy, and maybe I am. She has her heart in the right place, I suppose. But why construct a life out of duty? Why live to fulfill somebody else's expectations? Why sit on obligation like it's a golden egg? That shit doesn't get you anywhere. Enough.

They can call me hippie-dippie until the cows come home. I am my own man. I find my way fine. I rule the day, on my own terms.

I'm thinking about all of this—choiceschoiceschoices—as I zone out in front of the flickering images of late night chatter. I'm too buzzed to concentrate on any one thing. Good thing the ladies are off.

Someday I'll move out of this place, I think. Shelley will miss me then. I'm more unique that most.

THE PHONE CALL comes early. Eleven-forty eight. Too early to deal, but for some reason I pick up. I'm in the middle of a half-dream revolving around a slipper-clad electrician operating on my long-dead cat.

"It's your mother," she says. "I have some shocking news."

"Mhmmm," I say.

"It's Cheryl." She's crying. I sit up.

"What?"

She tells me everything: the car flipping on a wet hair-trigger turn, country road. The shock-trauma bolt to the hospital, last-ditch surgery attempt. All this last night—right after we talked.

"I'm headed there now. I need to help," she says. "There's so much to do. My God, those poor children."

"Jesus."

"*Will you.*"

"Sorry."

"I'll call. I'm assuming a funeral in a few days. I'll call."

"Okay," I say, but the line is already dead.

Shit, I think. The kickball game.

"SO, YOU'RE GOING, right?"

Gretchen sits smoking. I wished she did this post-coital rather than pre-coital. But I am surrounded by strong women. Perhaps this is as a result, I think, of having a feeble father figure. I don't know. Let the Freudians figure it out.

"I don't know," I say. "I have the kickball game. *You know*."

"You're kidding me, right? Wesley, you *have* to go to your aunt's funeral."

"We weren't close."

She shakes her head. Fountains of hair cascade into her eyes.

"No. No. You don't get it. She's your mother's sister, Wesley. You go for your *mother*."

"I can't believe I have to verbalize this. Your mother doesn't even like me."

I'm flipping through my D&D book, looking for a suitable "final stage" monster for my night as Dungeon master. Next week. I'm thinking King of the Bugbears.

"She doesn't not like you," I say.

"Two negatives does not equal a positive," she says.

"She doesn't like my 'lifestyle,' or so she calls it. I hate that word. 'Lifestyle.'"

"You're a *grown* man."

I'm in the dragon section, leafing through my options—nice illustration of the cloud dragon.

"I'm thirty-four and unmarried. And polyamorous—a word I could never utter around her. And she wants me to be a father of three so that she can cuddle with her grandkids."

I wonder if we have any grass left.

"If I go will you?" She smiles at me seductively. In her own gruff way, Gretchen likes to keep the peace.

"Let me think about it."

Gretchen puffs the hair from her face.

WHEN I'm out at sword-fighting, my mother leaves a message.

"What a tragedy. So sad what has happened here. Everybody is really at a loss for words. I know I am. At any rate, you may want me to inform you about the memorial service at this point. It's on Saturday at one o'clock. I'm sure I'll see you there. Please call and we'll figure out arrangements. Hugs and kisses. Talk to you soon."

I sit there drinking a beer in the half-light. Fading day.

Willow is sitting in front of me, topless. Umbros and Tivos on her feet. Her right nipple is pierced, slightly off-center. She's painting her toenails purple, listening to me carry-on.

"I don't know, baby. You tell me what I should say."

"I don't know, either. It's a principle, is all I'm saying. I just don't want to, I don't know, whore myself out to my family on a whim."

"Baby, it's a funeral. Ya know? They happen."

Fuck, I think. Rule the day.

I'm watching highlights of the X games. They have some goofy interlude. A guy dressed as a mastodon is doing an aerial flip on his motocross. His front and rear tires land just so, perfecto. The trunk flails. How do you do that? I wonder. There are strange talents out there.

"I don't think I'm telling you want you want to hear," Willow says, not looking up.

I wonder if I have any grass left.

"Wow," I say. Watching more X games. "That's something there."

I FALL ASLEEP in front of the TV. More exhausted than I knew. Willow falls asleep upstairs, lap top in the crook of her arm, cereal bowl next to her. We were both too busy for sex. Such is life.

I think I need to maybe set Willow free. Two is enough, maybe.

I wake up at three-thirty eight and go up to bed, lie down next to Willow anyway. She feels birdlike next to me, tiny frame.

"I'm not going," I tell her. She's sound asleep. It's better this way. "It's against my religion."

I think of my Aunt Cheryl. Like my mother she grew up in semi-austerity. But then everything changed. Her father—my grandfather—struck it rich in the stock boom (great investor). My mother and her children grew up within this nexus of affluence. So we've all benefitted.

Cheryl was the most generous—giving much of her wealth away to charity. This bred resentment, or so I've heard. She was beneficent. A good egg.

I'm lying there at four in the morning next to a twenty-two year old woman I don't really know beyond the body fluids we occasionally exchange and I'm recalling sitting in the back seat of Cheryl's van listening to James Taylor sing about Carolina as she mouths along. Over the mountains we rode and the highway glistened by—bits of rock and glass and asphalt and metal gleaming in the sunlight.

"We're going to have so much fun on this trip," she said in between songs on the tape deck.

And we did. Family vacation in a wood cabin—roasting marshmallows and fishing and chopping wood with a rusty hatchet and hiking through the stands of saplings whistling John Denver.

I bite my tongue in nostalgia. I lie face down in the pillow. I stifle everything.

"Mom." There are cracking sounds on the line. "I got your message, thank you so much. I'm trying to get a ticket out there, but I'm having some trouble. So, we'll see how I do. I'll call you if I'm able to get a ticket. But you know, if not, please send Uncle Gilbert my love and the kids, of course. It is a real tragedy. I'm so so sorry. Anyway, I'll talk to you soon. I guess."

It's twelve-fourteen. The funeral is tomorrow, as is the kickball game. I'd told my captain I'll be there. It's only the third game of the season after all.

I put the cordless back on the receiver and send Candi a text.

"Cum on over," she replies with a smiley face. I need to lose myself. Demon Warrior or sex or both.

I text Willow that we're through. No reply. I text Gretchen that I'll be in town this weekend—I don't mention Aunt Cheryl. I send Candi a smiley emoticon. She says she'll swing by at four.

I drink some chocolate milk straight from the jug.

Standing in front of the fridge, I eat three slices of American cheese, unwrapping each one carefully. I drop the empty plastic sleeves on the floor. Life is too short.

Standing over the sink, I eat a bag full of cheesy poofs. I don't want to get neon orange dust all over my "Fuck Yeah!" t-shirt. I got that in Atlantic City for five bucks—a real coup.

K

☞

TODAY she's taking me back. It's her chewing an apple, holding a poodle in the crook of her arm. Italian wears a blue hoodie, head up-turned. A tendril of hair falls on her nose, but she doesn't care. She's mid-bite into the Fuji. She's wearing a sailor shirt—blue and white striped. This is from several years ago. You can tell because her nose is narrower. You can tell because her lips are ever so slightly thicker. This is before we met. This is before everything important happened. It doesn't register. It's still her, but it's a previous her. The lockers in the background tell me I can't. The locker slats, as if they need to breathe. I'll wait until tomorrow.

Now this one she used before. This is a golden nugget from the archives of K. If I dared, I could see it all the time. If she deigned to accept me, that is. This is from last summer. Trip with Mamma Bear. It appears to be King's Dominion or Six Flags. Wide expanse of brick and stone behind them—the kind you see in entranceways to these places. A group of adolescent boys meanders behind left. A harried woman in an olive green hat brushes by far right. I don't look at them or Post-it them out. Mama Bear smiles on the right. She wears pink wire bunny ears. She has a nice smile. The genes are ap-parent. Same hair, tall. But I Post-it her out, anyway. She doesn't count. K, on the other hand, *counts*. Let's start with the pink bunny ears. Let's start with the index finger in her mouth, as if to say "oops," I forgot my _____. Her little finger dangles there, hook-like. But—as is nearly always the case—it's her eyes that keep me fixed. They are huge and blue and the eye whites are just as huge as the irises and they pop out at me from where they sit frozen in time and they draw me in and net me. I won't mention the reddish tinge (not even a tinge, more like a ringlet) of her hair or the rubber band around her wrist (is this to remind her of something)? I don't have to even remove the leather and I don't make a gesture to. It's better this way. Sticky-notes up. K there, finger in mouth. Me. Door closed.

K doesn't remind me of her in the least. That's the beauty of it. Today's update is simple aqua blue background. Wet pool hair. Massive blue eyes. Smile. Little bikini top—somewhat revealing, but certainly not slutty. We're at the aquarium today, perhaps? It can't be a waterfall (too light) or a bathroom wallpaper (too bright). It's clean and simple. No sticky-notes required. She's away now. Best for all concerned. Separation is the best maneuver we ever rigged. We were always in conspiracy together against ourselves. A marriage of convenience, perhaps. She wanted acceptance—her mother, her family, her friends, her church, her rivals. I wanted stability after far too many nights. Endless nights. Most years were years of nights. I often never saw the sun. K seems to live in it. The sun, I mean. One of her friends remarked, "Oh, you're so tan! You changed races." She does. She's different every time.

Slow day. Same image. I could go to my own private archives-in-the-making in a pinch, but I decide against it. Click away.

No change. Again. This is so unlike her. She must be busy at the Federal Grill. I bet she's a very busy girl. Perhaps her classes require too much of her. Perhaps her classmates should help her out more, so she can post. Certain things are more important. I wonder if K has any inclination. If she saw me I wonder what she would think or say. There is nothing wrong with me, I know. She would think the same thing, I'm sure.

Every time I decide I will click it. I don't click it. Someday I will click it and she'll see me as I am.

The first was unmemorable. I walked into the store. I was looking for gravel for my fish tank. And fish food. "Welcome to Fluffies. May I be of assistance?" She didn't look up from her *Cosmo*. She wore her hair up, which made her nose appear longer than usual. This was appealing. I like an aquiline nose. At first I thought the other girl in the back—the one stocking dog food—I thought she might be. But then she was too, almost too perfecto. Too put-together. I don't want perfecto. I want perfecto with a little messiness, something to hang my hat upon. I handed K the requisite money. Her fingernails clipped mine as she handed me two quarters, a dime, and a penny. I keep the coins in a plastic case in the box in the place where I keep such things. Her fingernail polish reminded me of watermelon flesh. I could see my reflection in her fingers. I noticed the twin marks—though they were not deemed as such then. She has just above her right lip a medium freckle—not a mole—and about an inch or two to the left, under her left nostril, another perfect freckle, even more delectable than the other. Even then, in the days before K became *K,* I knew this was alluring and special. "Have a nice day," she said. Her smile seemed to go *through* me. "You as well," I mumbled. Her eyes dropped back to her magazine, flipping pages. I said goodbye to her huge, amazing eyes. They were the size of silver dollars, lemons, medals, moons.

Ordinarily this would be one. But I can't see beyond the kid. She's smooching her little brother, schnoz pressed into his cheek, her eyes closed, hair bereted and layered with that beadwork thingie she is partial to. I can't sticky-note him. His mere presence betters me. It's not right. I'm pissed at K. "No kids!" I say. She does not hear me. Otherwise, this would be a good one. She's nearly coming out of her bathing suit—the sunflower and pineapple and paisley one. She wears two rings on her left hand. She wears aqua nail polish, which matches her suit (always so meticulous—I admire this). Her eyes are closed. It's as if I am the kid and she's the big sister. Despite the skin, you can't see it. It's a safety zone. I'm pissed at K. I go to the archives and finish there.

She updates well. This one reason. Today is not one, though from a different angle it could be. If she did something about the weird black-rimmed glasses and tidied up her helmet hair, it could be one. Youth is wasted by beauty. It's the helmet hair that stops me. Popcorn maker behind her, she sandwiches some guy in red. Baseball cap and stupid smile. Pink skin. Cargo pants. K wears white and she looks bigger up-top, which I can take or leave (I usually like medium-small). Sash rather than belt. Tan. Tan. Tan. Broken down boxes and tile. Somebody works there. This could become one. I'll save and revisit. I see promise.

It's been days without income. I need income. For electricity. For K. She wants me to occupy myself. I can feel the energy. So I answer the e-mails I go to the dreaded postal service. K needs to push me because if I fail to go to the dreaded postal service, they complain. If they complain, my rating goes down. If my rating goes down, I'm out. At least until I re-register via proxy. I decide to restrain myself from checking in on K. But then after the postal service, I do anyway. Luckily, it's demure K today. She's on the bleachers with the Italian and a plain Jane I don't know. She wears long-sleeves and cargo-pants and her binder sits next to her, covered with drawings. The sun catches her hair just so and she smiles with such aplomb. Little dimples. Lovely. We do not choose the object. It chooses us.

We walk together down a wooden glen. We begin from the position where it was taken—the wildflowers, the forested mountains (deciduous). The angle of the sun puts her almost in relief. Her hair blows in the wind and curls slightly from the humidity. I smell something—sassafras or honeydew or jasmine? Her scent or the delicate scent of the flowers and grasses, I'm not sure. She doesn't offer her touch quite yet. She leads me through the sunshine first. I can feel it through my shirt. My head feels warm, slightly dizzy. She walks one shoulder ahead. She knows the place. K. Under the boughs the air itself is cooler, as if the mouth of a cave. We enter the mouth and proceed into the throat and then amble forward behind the thicker trunks where the other campers can't see. We don't desire to get her in trouble. She has me recline there, on the soft pine needles, in the sweatless arbor.

Separator calls, but I let it ring through. I know she wants a progress report. She wants to monitor my ability to move forward. I am not concerned, nor do I care to elaborate one way or another. Also, I am involved communing with K. Priorities first.

K drives me mad with a simple glint and pucker. In this one today I cannot even see ninety percent of her eyes. Only the dusky shadow of them through her sunglasses. K was traveling—I had forgotten. She had the family reunion. She holds her hand up—the means by which she can capture herself so well. The brick facade of some business behind her. Her nose looks even wider now—even more alluring, not less. It's flared. Her imperfect nose is one of K's greatest assets. It separates her from the others. She is unique, and I'm sure she would appreciate my admiration. But what makes this one is the pursing of her lips, the come-hither tang, the V of a necklace slicing down into the brown of her hippie-dippie blouse. The leather falls to the floor. As does the denim. Some things cannot be helped.

The second time we met was back at Fluffies. I thought about her. I had to return for face time. The bell belled and I was in. Silent inside save for the burling tanks and the whoosh of air conditioning. "Hi, welcome to Fluffies." She didn't look up. She was texting. Her hair was up in some kind of Princess Leia thing. "Greetings," I said. "Do you recall our first meeting? You gave me some change." She stopped texting at that, and her eyes lifted. I wasn't trying to be rude, or to interrupt her perfectly natural socializing. I'm sure she was struck, dare I say blindsided, by my pheromones. "I don't know. Should I?" I told her I bought fish food and gravel. She raised her eyebrows and dropped back into her texting. "Lots of people buy those things. If I messed up or gave you the wrong change or something, don't tell my manager, okay? I'm already, like, in hot water." The thought of K in delightful hot water! I tried another tact. "How old are you?" She lifted her head and blushed slightly, despite her olive complexion. "How old do you *think* I am?" "A sophisticated age. Perhaps twenty-five?" "Too high, but thanks for trying." It was purposefully too high. She might have seen through it. "So, you're Kylie." She nodded, yawned. "What is your last name though?" She stared at me for a beat, considering her options. I was being brazen, far more brazen than I thought I might be. "Can I help you with some *pet products*?" I told her I'm looking for a Green-Eyed Blazer (made up, first thing I could think of). Just a generic fish. I wanted to drag this out as long as I could as far as I could. I wanted more eye time. "Let me check in the back for a moment," she said. "We have some new ones." But she never returned. It was her manager, "Glenda," who returned in her place. Glenda was not one for me. "Sorry sir, we don't have that particular fish. Is there something else I can help you with?" I decided to wait another day. There's always another day for sweet K.

She's on her prom picture. At least it most clearly appears to be the prom. Her dress is bright pink and she's wearing a corsage on her wrist and gold hoop earrings—which are the only instance of these I've seen. I sticky note her date, of course, but not before judging him. He has dark hair and a stupid smirk on his face, as if he just got away with something. Which he did. He's with K. Her smile is sardonic. Or ironic. Or ironically caustic. I can tell he's only on his arm because he was the best of some bad options. My K is picky (thankfully so). Her hands rest on his shoulders. But lightly puppy-like. He will not see what is underneath the pink curtain.

I stopped going to Fluffies. I wanted to. I knew she was *there*. I wanted to so badly. Just the image of Fluffies in my mind could send me. But I didn't dare. I did find out her last name using the website. This helped a lot.

Then she blocked me. She must have blocked me. I sat there typing in "K," as usual. She wasn't there. Nothing. I paced and paced and checked again. I paced and drank coffee and checked again. I told myself, no I will not check again, then I checked again. I told myself there is nothing in this world I would like more than a single photo, a mere reemergence. Then I checked again. Nothing.

I contemplated Fluffies again. I could always return and see if anything occurred. I was concerned, as a citizen of the community. I wanted what was best for her. I decided to e-mail them, inquire as to her well-being.

Three tortuous days later I received a reply stating that K no longer was employed at Fluffies. I drank a bottle of wine. I drank a beer. I fretted. I drank two shots of tequila. I drank two more glasses of wine.

I am fortunate for my in-case-of-emergency-archive. That is what I have. This qualifies as an emergency. I had her jumping out of a box with a two piece. I had her tongue out, receiving a strawberry as an offering. I had her at the club with bluish purple tights and dolled-up hair. I had her in front of her house hair just so, dipping down into her face. The light seems to be late evening. Pinkish-tan-nish shoes and belt. Bottle of water. This is, I bet, her favorite picture. Her nose looks smaller, her profile classic beauty. We still have a relationship.

In the winter, K wants to cuddle by the fire. She enjoys downhill skiing and I'm game for a few runs, though I can't stay on my feet. She's little and young, low center of gravity. She likes the daring-do aspects of it. She's impressed that I'm open-minded. So am I. Later she will compromise and we'll head down the flat cross-country trail—more my speed. She'll pretend not to be bored and will tell me how much I mean to her life. We'll eat at the lodge restaurant. She'll order the salmon because she's trying to stay slender. Her dimples dimple even more. We reminisce about previous trips we took. We reminisce about movies we've seen. We discuss mutual friends. It's sweet. After dessert (chocolate mousse for me, strawberry shortcake for her) we go upstairs. We hold hands. I remember when I proposed to her, on one knee, tears streaming down our faces. I kiss her ears first, and click the hotel door behind us. It's so beautiful. My eyes are closed.

In the morning, I drink my coffee and stare out the window. I am fifty-nine years old. Nobody in the world loves me. There's nobody.

MERE MORTALS

CHAD IS LUGGING the remnants of his wet bar. Stools. Also, a rotten picnic table and fence posts. Hefty bags filled with sticks and leaves. His wife loves Dumpster Day. She's at home readying another load. Chad's with her step-sister, Paula. She's wearing hip-huggers and a sun-yellow tank top. He tries not to gawp directly. Paula is twenty-seven and talks a blue streak. It's a plus.

—Whatever happened to sleaziness? I mean, real life sleaziness? Chad says.

—There's plenty. What are you *talking* about? What about all those movies? And the rock guys who make pornos? And the politicians? I mean, they can't keep their flies up.

—That's different. They're not real. Not really real.

—They are real. They have *families*.

Some do. Some don't. Chad tosses a moldering stool into the Dumpster. Paula drags a heavy bag of leaves, snailing a leaf skid.

—Yes, but they're entertainers on some level. They're famous. Or if not famous, at least known. They're on TV, Chad says.

—Okay. So?

—What, I mean is, the kind of cheating and carrying on that was commonplace in the 70's when I was growing up. You know, the stuff from those Updike stories.

—Up-who?

—I guess you're too young. Chad says.

Chad sniffs. Chad usually sniffs when his conception of someone is thrown for a loop. This is a minor loop-throw.

—You always say that. Paula claps the cuff of his flannel shirt.

He knows this is flirtatious. He also knows he can never act upon it.

—It always stinks around here, he says.

—It's a Dumpster, Chad. It contains *trash*.

—But it's not even in this area. A hundred yards over there it still stinks. It must be a sewage thing, or something.

He realizes he says this as an implicit way to deaden the sexual tension he established. He also realizes he sounds idiotic. He'll take the risk. They lean back toward the station wagon for more trash. If only he were single...rather than married to Paula's step-sister. He has more *fun* with Paula, that's for sure.

—I'm sure, Paula says.

Somewhere in America a man and a woman are cheating, doing something lascivious. Aren't they? He reads about this all the time.

—Don't worry, she says. People are getting divorced all the time.

This jolts Chad awake. He wasn't expecting this level of frankness.

—For sex?

—Anecdotal evidence, I guess.

Chad chucks part of the rotten picnic table into the Dumpster. Paula grabs a fence post.

—Celebrities thrive on sleaziness, she continues. Politicians, too. It's oxygen to them. Or at least to the tabloids which make them possible.

—That's true.

—It's a contrast is all. Between them and us.

They grab the rest of the stools, bags. The Dumpster seems bottomless.

Chad wonders—what is the worst that could happen? She would be mighty angry, but she wouldn't divorce him. She is constitutionally opposed, she said. Doesn't this give him a window of opportunity?

—I guess you're right. All those Paris Hilton types now all have their own sex tapes. It's viewed as a highway to stardom, or something. I get it.

—Have you ever seen any of those?

A pause.

Paula snorts. Chad does the same, coughing.

—Nothing could be less sexy, Paula says, not showing her hand. Paris Hilton was more interested in the camera than the dude.

—Yup.

—The Kim Kardashian one put me to sleep.

And then she does show her hand. Toothy, sheepish smile.

—Me too.

—Then there are these—what's the chick's name on E?

—I forget.

—But you know who I mean?

—Yeah.

—She's a celebrity parasite, a starlet feeding on gossip about the stars. A star (or starlet) in her own right, just because she's sucking on the blood of the stars.

—Yeah, he says.

They unload the remainder of the trash from the back of the station wagon. It's early. Birds chip in the maple stands. The sun shotguns through the leaves.

—They're like the Greek gods cavorting while we mere mortals look on in adulation, Chad continues.

—It's pretty amazing. This is how we have evolved.

—Or devolved.

—Devolved.

They sit in the car. He rolls down his window. He waits to see if another Dumpster Day car will come. It's stupid really—it's just a day (however advertised) to throw shit out.

He can imagine the family reaction. Your wife's step-sister? C'mon. You can't be serious? What a filthy dirtball. He'd be castigated. Or worse.

How does anyone handle witnessing their reputation dragged so sloppily through the mud?

And yet.

—I think she's probably waiting for us, Paula says.

His cue. Her hand drops to her tanned thigh, slides up. Hers mirrors his.

—Yeah, you're right.

There is so much more he'd like to say. He'll replace saying with doing when Paula is not at home waiting for them to return. Justifications are easy; endings never are. But save this for later, he thinks. The pain will come later. Delay the gratification; that's the best part.

He starts the ignition. The Doors on the radio—"Break on through to the other side."

He'll let his wife take the next run with Paula. He could use a cold drink or cigarette or both. If only he knew how to smoke.

COUPLETIME!

☛

BLOTCHES OF RAIN splotch the windshield. Wipers smear them silly. The satellite radio is out. Forgot to pay the bill. Should've gone automatic billing. Have to pull the vehicle over. Needs more oil. Something is wrong, that's for sure. Gracie is unamused, or I *think* she is. It could be sarcasm. Irony? She's younger than me, so sometimes I misread her. Sometimes I'm not as astute as I could be in the all-important street smarts category.

"It's fine, Gil," she says. "Don't worry."

And she seems earnest. She's smiling true. It's *my* smile. It's the one that says *relax*. But, how can I? It's the one that says you're being ridici. But am I? Do I distrust too easily? The worst usually *does* happen, eventually.

I'm under the hood, capping the engine. I'm watching oil drip from underneath. Like a mechanical udder.

I wish I knew how to fix one damn thing in life. I'd be a better person than I am.

Sweat sops my shirt.

"Screw it," I say and let the hood drop. "Let's go to Middleton." We're only eleven point six miles away.

ONCE A MONTH we do these little getaways. We drive an hour. We drive two. It's Coupletime! It's time to bond, to coalesce. It's important for our relationship. We've made agreements. We've made compromises. We stay away from big cities. We stay away from corporate America. It has to be small towny or rural. Quaint. We're striving for authenticity. We're trying to purchase realness. We're trying to find our true selves in quilted America. Bonding.

Problem is only so many rural enclaves and small towns within a few hours. We've hit most of them. If we wanted to be obnoxious and self-aware, we could blog. We could pitch a book to some boutique press.

So, we are on repeats now. Unavoidable. We have a rotation.

Gracie likes this, says it brings back the warm memories. She says each experience is its own thing. Different seasons. Different people. Different aspirations. Moods.

I don't like the second time around. It's almost, without exception, disappointing. This goes for movies, restaurants, lovers. The novelty of discovery *is* the pleasure.

Gracie calls me neurotic.

"No," I say. "Just smart."

"If only."

BUT I'M RIGHT about the second time through.

To wit: we arrive at the Red Fox Inn, a B&B just off Main Street Middleton. Last time we stayed at the Horse and Stable, which was small and truly charming and perfect. This time we thought the Red Fox would/could be a bit of an upgrade. It's *not* an upgrade.

The "innkeeper" wearing a red and gold uniform, which smacks of hotelery cliché (Gracie disagrees), takes us to our room, which is new and comes equipped with a flat screen and an HVAC and a rug featuring little macaroni patterns in "tasteful" maroon and burnt orange on a field of Kelly green.

This does not strike me as authentic or quaint. It strikes me as overly calculated.

I'm immediately considering cancellation.

We can't without paying for the room.

"Can you remove the television?"

"Is there a problem with the television?"

"I'm sure it's a fine television. We just would like to read."

"Yes, sir. I see. However, perhaps you may want to watch television at some point during your stay? It does also play music."

"No. We don't watch television."

"Is it a problem to keep the television and simply leave it off?"

"Yes, it is," I say. "It's distracting."

So, then we have to go through this entire rigmarole about the television in which I become defensive and she becomes—what?—insistent or bristling?

Gracie interrupts and says we'll just take the room as is.

"Let it go," she says. "We can ignore the television."

"*You* can," I say. "I cannot."

"Then I will ignore the television. You can practice working on that area of your personality."

Which is true.

SEE, the last B&B in which we stayed was perfecto in every way. Pineapple wallpaper. Quilts on the bed. Quilts on the walls. Little framed mini-quilts on the doors. Little carved wooden men on little carved wooden shelves. Victorian gables and peaks and creaky wooden stairs and floors. Lace and silk and whatnot.

We had perfecto candlelit dinners with wine from the local wineries. Artisan everything. Pork chops with little dollops of mango chutney and cilantro and chives sprinkled just so. Sweet potato mash. Fried organic tomatoes. Blueberry/blackberry pie a la mode.

We scoured the local wineries, which were (I have to admit) perfecto. The weather was dry and cool. The air was filled with beneficent tidings. Birds chirped playfully from the bush, but failed to dive-bomb us or shit in our hair. I noticed the absence of conflict.

And the wines tasted of chinaberry and cantaloupe and hints of chocolate or Craisins or barbecue flavored Fritos or whatnot. And the ladies who dispensed the wine were pretty and sweet and played with the tendrils of their hair just enough to seem flirtatious, but not enough to measure as any kind of threat to Gracie (at least not stated). The result was buzzy lovemaking with just a hint of possessiveness—as instigated by the casual flirtations. Yes, the quilts took something away from the sensuality of the moment for me. No, I wouldn't have objected to the presence of one or more of the wine scags in the room—either watching or joining in. However, all in all, the previous trip was a certain A.

SECOND TIME around. B&B corporate. We are at odds over how much to confront them or just let it be.

"Let's relax, okay?"

I tell her I can't relax if the place has bad juju, or whatnot.

"Wasn't expecting televisions and all," I say. "This is to get a break from that."

I want to confront her about her lack of validation for my perfectionistic nitpicking.

"I'm tired," she says. Curls away from me. There was no curling away from me last time.

I try to renegotiate. Change the mood before I sour it completely. Let it go, as advised.

"Your hair looks very nice," I say. I feel absurd kowtowing.

She nods, head away from me.

Then we don't say anything for a while.

"Where would you like to go for dinner? What are you feeling like?"

She shrugs. Wherever.

"A burger or something is fine," she says.

She never wants a burger. Worse, a burger means giving up on romantic/sexual aspirations. It means a restaurant which plays "More Than a Feeling" as background music.

So, WE EAT BURGERS at a mid-tier place, one half-step up from bar food. Really, glorified bar food, in actuality.

I eat fries and a Caesar salad along with my "elk burger." This is how quickly the weekend has gone south. We talk about her friend, Carmen, who is involved with a man twice her age. I protest.

"Kinda gross, isn't it?"

"Why are you so judgey all of a sudden?"

"We're just talking."

"You're older than *me*, in case you forgot."

"No, I haven't. You won't let me."

"You *are* older than me."

"But not that much older."

"What's the difference really?"

I eat my (non-artisanal) French fries.

A low point.

The second time around is never as good as the first.

We skip dessert.

LEST I FORGET—it rains the entire weekend. During the TV debate, during dinner, during post-dinner walk-around time, during the winery fiascos—raining blobby disgusting, oily splotches of rain all over us. The entire time. On this coupledom Mecca—or so it has been touted—raining. Pissing rain.

We speed-walk down Main Street from the burger place down past the dressage stores, past the country squire shops, past the bookstores featuring leather bound tomes, past the antiquey knick-knack shops.

One of these stores has an autumn harvest display. Scarecrow and pumpkins and gourds and the like. Fancified. As we walk past, a mouse crawls out of the scarecrow eyehole and skitters across the fancy pants store. It's perfect. The best moment of the weekend.

THAT NIGHT we watch some kind of antique roadshow on television. Gracie doesn't feel like much else, she says. We don't drink wine or champagne or cuddle or read or listen to music. We watch the screen. We don't screw. It's as if we never left home.

In the morning we eat frozen bagels and prune juice. They are out of coffee so we drink weak tea. Yum. They are out of orange juice so we drink water. I ask if they have cream cheese, but all they have is margarine.

We shower and dress and drive to the winery number one—or try to, but the car is completely out of oil so we have to call Triple A to come out. Two hours later they finally do, only to tell us what we already fucking know, which is that our car has a leaky oil tank.

"You should get that looked at," the guy says.

"Thanks a million," I say. I try to not make it sound sarcastic.

We take the Cork Shuttle instead. The Cork Shuttle is filled with (already) drunken ex-sorority types with tans and ankle bracelets and those stupid plastic wrist things. They drink wine from plastic glasses or straight from the bottle and gnaw on little wedges of organic smoked Gouda and water crackers.

Gracie and I sit in the back.

"Hey, don't you two wanna have some fun?" One of the sorority types chortles before we even get to the first winery.

"No," I say. "Not particularly."

They take me seriously, but the upside is: there is more us from that point forward. A good thing.

The wine tastes vinegary at the first one and there's an odd poo smell wafting from the vineyard.

"Do vineyards use cow manure?" I ask Gracie.

She bobs her head and says she doesn't smell anything.

"It's all natural. Relax."

I am told to relax often.

The second one has a wide assortment of fruity sweet dessert wines—which all taste like liquefied jam to me, in essence.

The sorority ladies are toasted.

In the Cork Shuttle one moley-faced woman vomits on my pants, then—in an attempt to clean up—smears it around with some tissue paper she withdraws from her purse.

"That's okay," I say. "I'll keep the memory safe."

The third winery won't let me in as a result of my funkified pants. They let the puker in, however, no sweat.

"If you have a paper apron on or something," I say. "I can change into that."

"We're not a hospital ward," she says. "Hospital" makes the point, I think.

"I mean, I'm sure you've had this happen before," I say. "Accidents do happen."

"It's a first, actually," the woman says. "I have to say."

She's one of those overly dimply Jennifer Garner types—perky and annoying (though she *thinks* she's Victoria's Secret material). And affixed with too much cheap, hippie-dippie jewelry for my taste.

"I don't have much to look at anyway," I say.

Gracie is already inside slurping her wine with the overgrown sorority girls.

Dimples sashays off.

I find a prime spot and take a crap in the vineyard for any and all to witness.

Gracie has to bail me out of the county clink that afternoon. Using a cab.

THE SECOND go round is always a stale imitation of the first. I try to recapture the glory of the discovery and fail miserably. I try to place why I fell in love with experience X initially, but like an amnesiac, I can't remember the trigger or can't pull the trigger, or can't find the worm hole.

Day two we left for horse-back riding and mountain climbing. The mountain is a mere foothill, but it was something we didn't have a chance to explore last time. I spent the morning—after a breakfast of stale powdered donuts, tea, and a brown banana—at the gas station getting my oil tank or whatnot, patched. Nine hundred and eighty-seven dollars and three plus hours later, I have my car back.

We drive out to the hill. It really is a hill, not a mountain, and if I had a chance to verbalize the difference to the promoters of Middleton proper, I would do so. Hills roll, mountains climb. This rolled. But, whatever. I was hoping to one day have sex with my wife again. The romantic getaway was hurting, not helping. We climbed the hill and I smiled and I didn't complain and I tried to think positive thoughts. The rain stopped, which helped, though the mud was bad enough to turn most of the bottom third of my pants brown. Gracie's also.

Onto the horsies.

What we couldn't predict was the fact that the horse farm we found on the web was only for *purchasing* bred horses, not for taking a horse out on a spin. It was a horse dealership of sorts. This was to Gracie's great dismay.

"Just wondering, is there a place where we can, you know, ride horses? There are horses everywhere in Middleton."

"That is very true, but not that I know of. There used to be one, but I think it went out of business a decade ago."

"So that's a no."

"Sorry."

Fuck me. I'm still smiling to mollify the bonding. Horses everywhere, but none to ride. This place is a horsey dick tease.

"It's okay," Gracie says. "Life happens."

This is generous on her part.

I have an insecure fixation with playing the host on these kinds of trips, as if any blemish is entirely my fault. Not only do I want everything to be perfect, but I want everything to proceed according to my vision of it and I want any experiential blemish or boil to be subsumed by my ability to orchestrate the event or weekend just so.

Then a release: Gracie turns to me and says, "Why don't we just get out of here?"

It's almost as if the rain stops, the waters part, and the sun comes out as she says it.

"Okay," I say. Simple. After checking out we drive home into the sunlight. I wear my sunglasses. We smile without restraint.

We listen to music we love—the Beach Boys, Talking Heads, Elvis Costello.

When we pull into our neighborhood the oil light comes on. But I don't even care. I'll buy a new car or fix the old one again. As long as I don't have to go back to Middleton for a third time.

We bring our stuff in. We check the mail. We make love in the dark of our own bedroom. I never want to leave home again.

E-LICKS-SIR

☞

"*THAT'S* the name?"

"Isn't it great?"

Champ and Scott were drinking champagne and pineapple juice, spearing smoked salmon slices onto Melba toast with toothpicks. They were in the Savannah Room, congratulating. Celebrating. The walls were papered with grass. Champ sat on the Zebra chair. Scott smoked a cigarillo. Champ and Scott bent over Champ's laptop where the company logo filled the entire screen. Champ's laptop hummed quietly. It was the sound of evolvement. They were a start-up; they were *going somewhere.*

"It's good," Scott said. "I likey."

"No hesitations? You usually have hesitations? That's why we're here, to talk about any hesitations."

"Well...."

"Out with it." Champ was elbows on knees, eyebrows raised. He wasn't sure about this. He quit his job for this—albeit, it wasn't career track, but it wasn't shabby. His girlfriend said he was bonkers. So he dumped his girlfriend. Scott said they would be wealthy in two years.

"Licks? Isn't that a bit...something. Too tangy. Too homoerotic? Something."

"No, it *licks* the pain and suffering one may be feeling. It doesn't lick *sirs*."

"A little brash maybe. People may balk."

"No, they're not balking. They get it. Licking is a *positive* association. Who doesn't like licking?"

"Okay, you asked for hesitations though. It's not me balking on the licking. It's other people."

"Anything else?"

Scott scratched his leg through his maroon jump suit.

"Well, I mean the punctuation. Do we need all the hyphens? It looks complicated. People want simple."

"The hyphens mirror the flow of the elixir, see? It's a water thing."

"Oh, it's a water image."

Champ tapped the logo featuring a waterfall cascading down onto the arched back of a flying Pegasus and then continuing down to puddle at the feet of four dancing sprites circling a Maypole inside a bower reminiscent of a rainbow.

"That's nice," Scott said, impaling another salmon sliver. "Like the pumpernickel Melba. Nice touch."

Champ leaned his sizeable torso back and gritted his teeth, exhaled, then rocked forward again to face his partner.

"Look, you're in with twenty five percent, right?"

"Yes, I am."

"I'm the one taking the vast majority of risk here. You just relax, you know. Just drink bubbly, enjoy the moment."

"Would you like to hear any more hesitations?"

"More?"

"That's why we're here. Nothing is set in stone yet."

Champ waves his hand to indicate, c'mon, continue.

"Well, what I was saying about the hyphens is germane. You really don't want to distract the consumer from what's important. The first hyphen makes it sound as if our product is some kind of online energy drink. Virtual. Then the splattering of hyphens—it just seems overly heavy handed, you know. With the Pegasus *and* the fairies *and* the hyphens? It's too busy."

Champ shook his head as if Scott just insulted his mother.

"Just trust me, Scott. It'll be fine. And they're sprites, not fairies."

He hoped it would be fine. He wanted it to be fine. It would be fine.

TWO WEEKS LATER Champ received the first large shipment from Aardvark Industries. A week after that the website went live.

ELicksSir.com proclaimed: "The energy drink to beat all energy drinks! E-licks offers you the high energy of all the others. But unlike all the rest, E-Licks-Sir fills your emotional voids! We especially engineer E-Licks-Sir to internally correct any cavern in the human heart. Using only the highest quality Tibetan roots and herbs, E-Licks-Sir will conquer your personal Himalayans! Having a bad day at work? E-Licks-Sir will make your boss seem like George Clooney! Sad about your dog's bone cancer? E-Licks-Sir will make you feel light as a canary!"

After several days of tweaking the design, Champ was satisfied. Amber the intern sent out e-mails, promotional copy, press releases and bombarded social media (when she wasn't too exhausted from working nights at the retro country and western bar). She never complained about the Hillbilly clientele, she complained about the work load.

"How many times do I have to bend over slowly? I mean, what am I showing them that is so unique?" She traced her Willow Tree ankle tat with her thumb.

"Um," Champ said. "I'm not sure they are after novelty."

The orders began trickling in and Amber filled them. Then, once several health magazines gave positive reviews to E-Licks-Sir the orders became so numerous Champ had to bring another intern from Vinnie's Grill. Crystal was hardworking and dutiful and gave one hundred and ten percent.

Then when *Male Health* reviewed E-Licks-Sir positively the orders shot up even more.

Customers posted glowing comments on the "feedback" section.

—Fred from Lansing, MI: "My mother passed away two and a half years ago and I've been struggling with depression since. Therapy didn't help much. Then came along E-Licks-Sir. What a fountain of energy and hope I now feel! I'm offering bottes of your amazing nectar to all my friends and family for Christmas."

—Susan from Wilmington, DE: "Amazing stuff! I'm dying to know what your secret ingredients are. I've died and gone to heaven with E-Licks-Sir! I truly feel like the flying unicorn on your logo— bottled in delight!"

—Cheryl from Sacramento, CA: "I'm not one to usually partake of energy drinks for one reason or another, but when I heard about the emotional energy your product offered, I had to give it a shot. I am not longer an angry witch! Thank you for saving my marriage."

That night Champ celebrated in the Bayou Room with his interns: the tenderloin was especially tender. Amongst the images of flying frogs and crocodile they spooned foie gras into each other's mouths.

"To E-Licks-Sir," Champ said.

"E-Licks-Sir!" Amber and Crystal chimed in.

"Scott, I need your help," Champ said. He rarely left voice mail messages, but he was in a bad way. They were over five hundred orders behind: the girls alone couldn't keep up. Champ himself was doing some of their work, but he wasn't as fast or dexterous as they were. Champ could only fill maybe twenty an hour and that was with a full cup of coffee in his belly (he'd never drink a God-awful energy drink—who knows what's in that crap).

An hour later Scott still hadn't returned Champ's call.

"Christ on a cracker. Where *are* you, fucknob?"

The new orders were coming in almost faster than he could fill the old ones. Champ's fingers were bleeding.

Three hours later Scott finally called.

"Sorry, Champ. I was out."

"This is a damn cell phone."

"Yes it is. I had it turned off, sorry."

"I told you about that."

"It was personal. It was a family emergency."

Family emergency.

"Oh, well I hope Aunt Mabel's hangnail is okay now."

Scott got the gist of it and came right over.

It didn't matter. The pace of new orders far exceeded the pace of old order completion. Even with the interns and Scott helping Champ they ended up that night at 502—two more than they began the day with. This was happening, Champ knew. He was ready to celebrate. Anywhere but the hillbilly bar.

BY THE MORNING of the next day there were 1,026 orders.

"We need employees," Champ told Scott. They were filling orders as they ate breakfast.

"Yup," Scott admitted.

Champ drove down to the local 7-11 and hired ten Hondurans at seven dollars an hour.

"What do I feed these guys?" Champ asked.

"Nothing. The employer doesn't have to provide food. This is not a cafeteria."

"Good point."

The Hondurans worked fast and two days later they were down to 326 at close of business. By the next morning, however, they were back up to 1,089. The pace of purchase was picking up.

Then the *bad* reviews began trickling in:

—Jake from Columbus, New Hampshire: "I didn't feel any 'emotional uplift' from this snake oil. The bottle doesn't even list any ingredients. For all I know its dried milk and goat's piss. It tastes terrible, whatever it is. Stay away!"

—Cindy from Billston, SC: "No disrespect intended, this crap does nothing for me. It left me gassy and cramped actually. It tasted old."

—Kevin from Lakewood, OR: "What's with the two week delay? It's ridiculous for such a new product."

—David from Elliott, MD: "By the time my order showed up I was no longer sad."

—Phil from Edgewood, FL: "This and all energy drinks are a waste of money. Drink coffee instead. It tastes better and doesn't strip Tibet of its roots and herbs."

A WEEK LATER the orders all but stopped. It was as if a switch went off. That was it. They were donezo.

They went from two thousand plus a day down to thirteen. Then four.

Another week later Champ had to stop picking up the Hondurans. Nothing for them to do. Then he had to say goodbye to Crystal. Then, sadly, to Amber. He missed Amber as soon as she walked out the door.

He called Scott and requested a meeting in the Iguana Room. The terrariums. The camouflage print walls. The dark reptilian shadows.

"Doesn't look good," Scott said.

They drank lukewarm tea.

"Spare me the obvious. What's the root cause?"

Champ slunk his massive shoulders. His hands were the size of griddle pans. These rested on the arms of the black leather chair (he is still looking for a chair made of Monitor lizard).

"Who knows?" Scott said. "People are fickle as hell."

"Was it the bad reviews?"

"Maybe."

"Was it the God-damned name? Were you right about that? What changed?"

"Not vital. We *were* selling."

Scott told him. A customer discovered the "secret ingredients" and was blasting her all over the online chat boards. That's all it was. Scott only knew this himself because Amber confessed upon her dismissal. She was a true-blood health nut and wanted to share the wealth. Unfortunately, her sharing of the wealth made for no actual wealth.

"So what's so wrong with a little soy milk and caffeine?"

Scott shrugged.

"Jesus," Champ said. "How do we stop the bleeding?"

CHAMP THOUGHT about calling his old boss, begging and pleading. He couldn't do that—he knew he couldn't do that.

Champ thought about finding Amber, doing something he shouldn't do. He was pissed beyond belief. The expression seeing-red—Champ now understood the true meaning of that saying.

But after a few beers and some violent, herky-jerky driving around the county, Champ decided he'd cut his losses. After all, a company must move forward, must learn from its lessons. He filled the last few orders himself, shut down the website, donated the excess stock to charity. He called Aardvark Industries, the supplier, and canceled all future orders.

Scott dropped by to check on progress. He wore a mint green jump suit with red stripes down the arms.

"We still made a lot of money didn't we?"

Champ nodded. "We did okay for a few weeks."

They drank coffee and ate blueberry Danish with cream cheese.

They were in the Tangle Room. Ropes of hemp hung from the ceiling and draped down the walls.

"I have a new idea," Champ said.

"Oh no. No, no, no."

"The singing candle. It has a small iPod like thing implanted in the wax. This way you can have, you know, a romantic evening— the music, the candle. With this it's the music *in* the candle. One stop shopping."

"Terrible idea. Horrible. No more creative ideas."

"The only thing it doesn't do is fellate you."

"That's your job, asshole," Champ said. "I want my old life back."

Scott shrugged and backed out. He could find another partner, Champ knew. He had plenty of money to blow—silver spoon and all. For Champ, time for something else. Savings depleted, company deep-sixed. He smacked his face with his hand. This felt right, so he did it again and again. Eventually the blood came. "Idiot!" he shouted. "Idiot!"

He stopped there, but more was coming later. He knew that.

SHIT FLOWER

☛

"THEY CUT DOWN the last old growth tree in Virginia," Dirk says. "Just yesterday. Buzzed it to the ground. Turned it into toilet paper. I kid you not, it's public knowledge."

"Really? The last one?" Carol leans forward. They lean forward a lot, as if they really *care*.

The girls are on the bus, on the way to school.

"All that's left are trash trees. That's it. This was the last *real* tree. Arborists are pissed beyond belief and some are just quitting entirely—going to work at McDonald's or Arby's or something. Throwing themselves off a bridge. What's the point? The tree holocaust already happened. Might as well colonize Mars now. Ruin another planet."

Coffee with Carol—old grad school classmate from twenty years ago. They talk about their respective divorces, dealing with career disappointments. She's sweet and a bit overly needy, but Richard has always been able to really let loose in her presence.

"There is nothing," Dirk says. "Absolutely nothing. The job market today is worse than 1931 and nobody cares. We can all just shrivel up and die—it's fine."

It's validating.

Dirk thinks a lot of Carol—she saved him many times in grad school. Dirk gravitates towards warmth, since he can be disconnected and surly. He needs warmth. At least that's how *he* feels. Self-perception is a funny thing, he thinks.

They are at one of the last remaining bookstores in the city. Dirk knows the owner; also knows they are only still open because the owner has a sizable nest-egg from his years of corporate prostitution.

Dirk buys six books to provide support to the cause. On the way out, the bag slips from his hand and the books tumble directly from the bag into a sloppy puddle. All instantly ruined. Carol bears witness, arms crossed.

Unbelievable, Dirk thinks. He just shakes his head, picks up the bag of soggy books and drops the entire mess into the trash across the street. There goes that hundred and fifty dollar bill. It's not even nine a.m. and Dirk's day already blows chunks.

DIRK IS TEACHING his online class. "Teaching." He knows it's not the same. Mostly his online class entails posting canned information and assignments—and eventually grading them. Is that teaching? It's *related* to teaching, he supposes. He doesn't consider it such, but it pays the bills. Eventually, he thinks, it will all be automated anyway. All of it will. Robots will "teach" classes with links to Wikipedia and YouTube. Some automatic grading algorithm will take care of the back end—offering perfectly succinct comments to students along with line edits. Great, he thinks, just stick me on the curb with a sign around my neck. FREE, NEEDS GOOD HOME.

He stands up to fetch another cup of sour coffee, stubbing his right toe against the leg of his desk.

"Son of a bitch," he says, bounding.

It's probably broken. Perfect. Now he has a future ten thousand dollar operation, just because he was sleepy.

He drops ice cubes into a Ziploc baggie and wraps that around his throbbing toe.

Dirk e-mails a student who never capitalizes anything, not even his name. He's like the freaking bell hooks of the thirteenth grade.

Dirk sends the student a Google Image of a capital "I." Recognize this? Twit. He knows he can be a huge asshole, but there are standards. He considers putting the following policy on his syllabus: any usage of the lower case I will equal automatic failure from this composition course with an accompanying recommendation to return to second grade.

His toe is completely numb.

Things were once better. There once was sunshine and flowers. There was baseball and lemonade. There were swimming pools, watermelon, and cold beer. Now there is this throbbing toe and the lines on his face and billowing dread.

DIRK'S SISTER calls to discuss the upcoming family reunion. I don't get weekends, Dirk thinks. Just a different kind of work really. Family work. Unpaid work.

"You looking forward to Sunday?"

"Sure, why not?"

"Same here," she says.

"Alfred died," Dirk says. The Guinea pig. "The girls are devastated. I don't know what they expected. He's a freaking Guinea pig. They live only slightly longer than moths. But still. This is what I'm dealing with."

"I'm sorry for your loss."

"He smelled like dried fecal flakes, really. I mean, let's be honest here." They're laughing.

"Also, my fucking stairwell drain is clogged again. Every time it rains I'm out *in* the rain with a bucket. It's like a sewer just washed into my house."

"There's a solution to that problem," she says.

"I know. The solution is no more rain."

DIRK IS AT GROUNDS, his favorite coffee shop/café/knick-knack shop. No more stubbed toes here—let someone else do the work. He's up-dating his blog, ranting about the dearth of literacy in America. Rant-ing is breathing. "And we have too much smiling. Too much smiling, not enough reading. If you see me, don't you dare smile—go read a book! These people are starving. Don't be nice to me, go embrace a dying kid—you are to blame for the fact that he's dying, you know." As he's typing, he's thinking about the old bakery where his mother used to take him as a young boy. The bakery burned to the ground when he was a teenager—and it was as if his childhood also was in cinders. Smile about that!

He hears a snicker over his right shoulder. He cranes his neck.

"I'm sorry," the woman says, looking the other way, laughing into her hand. "I'm sorry. That's some funny shit."

"At least *you* read."

"Even if it's eavesdropping. Or the written equivalent thereof."

"I wasn't talking. Eavesdropping implies you're listening in." He doesn't mind. She might be his only reader of the day. Of the *month*.

She raises her glass.

"At least it's reading."

The woman has a mohawk dyed purple and orange. Her ears are each punctured by some twenty or twenty five earrings. Her ears re-mind Dirk of a deep sea fishing expedition. She's short and has vir-tually no neck, stubby little shoulders that look smushed and bludgeoned somehow.

"Amy," she says.

"Dirk."

"I fucking hate smiles. Don't smile."

"I promise not to smile."

"Thank you."

THEY GO for a walk down by the fetid canal. The smell is one third algal bloom, one third gasoline, one third moldering dead things. Dirk tells Amy about the divorce, about raising his two daughters as a single father, living in a tiny townhouse with walls so paper-thin he can frequently hear his neighbors snoring, belching, signing, farting, yawning.

"I have to wear ear-plugs to bed. In my own house. And I have the fan going full blast. How about you?"

"How about me, what?"

"What's your story?"

"I don't know. I'm just here. I live."

"Living is good."

"I was into art for a while. So, there's that. I guess you can tell that by looking at me. Art school type and all."

"Painter?"

"Woodblock prints, mostly. Pseudo-Japanese-inspired shit. I had a studio. It was just too hard to make it. The money, you know? But at least I'm trying and not doing some bullshit installation featuring a million marbles and feathers dumped randomly on the floor, or whatever. It is tempting though—the marbles and feathers."

Dirk likes the underbelly. She's got a façade as well, but he can sense a little teaspoon of softness. And she's not full of herself, which is refreshing.

"Did you stop?"

"I still work, but I have to pay the bills. I waitress. But tips aren't great really, as you might guess. Scraping by. I don't even like the word 'waitress' really. It sounds dismissive to me. 'Server'?" She shakes her head, world-weary. But no *way* is she as world-weary as him, he thinks.

Is it even possible to connect to another person? Dirk wonders this often. Is it a sleight of hand? Is someone just faking it? Is it possible to really "get" anybody? He feels like a goldfish swimming in a murky jar, alone. He wonders if he was always this despairing. He couldn't have been when he was fourteen and so easily ga-ga.

It starts to rain.

"Shit," Dirk says. "Of course, it rains." At least it is not raining snapping turtles. Or daggers.

"Well, we had a little walk."

Dirk knows he needs more purple-headed visionaries in his life.

The rain picks up, dousing them both. Pretty soon they're soaked.

IT IS STILL raining.

Dirk picks his daughters up from school. Iris is seven and Nellie is nine. Iris is the spunky one. Nellie is the quiet finger painter, who simply wants a room and quiet.

"Much homework tonight?"

"Nah," they both say. Homework has been made obsolete. Nobody wants to stress out the kids or yank them from their screen-addled coconuts.

"That's good. Rest up now while you have a chance. Pretty soon you'll be drowning in the stuff and hating your lives."

Nellie shrugs.

She's heard it all before, Dirk knows.

Nellie will take care of Iris. Iris will throw a tantrum over a knot of tangled hair or her sister's cross-eyed stare. They will play outside until it gets dark. He still has a ton of work to do editing the book for Sunflower Press. Mind-numbing copy-editing, mostly. An article here, a comma there. Scratches on the page.

Then he remembers the rain. They'll have to watch a movie—the eighty-fifth viewing of *The Little Mermaid*. Maybe *One Hundred and One Dalmatians* if he is lucky. Luckily he has both memorized—so he can block out the noise.

Apples and Doritos for snacks.

Chocolate milk with one ice cube in Nellie's, the way she likes it. Just one, like a frozen raft on the muddy Nile.

Amy calls at four-forty five, leaves a message. She wants to hang out later.

THE BASEMENT stairwell drain is clogged. Dirk remembers coming across the word "flood" in the Sunflower Press manuscript. Shit, shit, shit.

He bolts downstairs, but it's too late. The water is already all over the utility room, lapping against the shelf of vinyl records and vintage paperbacks. He tosses rags into the water and starts bailing out the stairwell maniacally. Noooooooooooooo! The records. The paperbacks are high enough off the ground that most are still dry, but the albums were all on the floor. He's going to have to trash them all.

This is my life, he thinks. Job. I'm fucking Job. My entire collection. What have I done to deserve this?

Once he gets the stairwell bailed out, he places a trash can over the clogged drain, so at least it catches the water.

He tosses the albums in a black Hefty bag. He could/should salvage the albums themselves, even if the cover art is destroyed, but, he figures, what's the point? Velvet Underground, Miles Davis, Rolling Stones, The Doors, The Animals, all down the bunged-up drain. What a moron I am, Dirk thinks. I saw this coming and did *nothing*. I deserve this. I totally deserve this.

THE GIRLS are wrapping up with *The* fucking *Little Mermaid* and Dirk is too flustered to return to work. Editing will have to wait. He opens a beer and a bag of peanuts and sits at the breakfast bar feeling sorry for himself. He downs the beer and opens another. He's relieved he's at least past that asinine "Under the Sea." If he hears that cock-a-doodle song *one* more time he's going to throw *himself* under the sea.

Then he remembers Amy.

Gives her a call.

He explains.

"What a shit storm," she says. "I'm sorry."

"I'm no good at taking care of this house. I'm not handy. It's just one more thing I have to think about. It's enough just trying to work and take care of the girls. You have kids?"

"No, I'm not good with them, for some reason. Even when I was a kid I wasn't good with kids."

"You want to come over tonight, later after the girls are down for the count? Watch a movie? Drink? Mostly drink."

"Of course."

His stubbed toe feels better already. Somehow.

HOT DOGS and roasted cauliflower—Iris is happy. More chocolate milk for Nellie. Orange juice for Iris. They chirp lines from *The Little Mermaid*. Bath time. Story time. Bed time. He tucks them in, night light on, bunk beds creaking.

Amy knocks on the front door an hour later.

They sit on the couch and drink margaritas from a frozen mix. Dirk is feeling it.

He puts on some old scratchy blues—what he listens to most of the time. One of the few albums that wasn't in the basement.

"I like this music," she says. "A lot."

"Blind Lemon Jefferson. All these guys had nothing, they were poor as hell and abused, and they made this incredible music. And now they are all-but-forgotten. Like a flower growing from a pile of shit. A shit flower."

Dirk likes Amy, but he feels awkward. It's been a long time. And he's not particularly attracted to her, still nursing his gamine Audrey Hepburn fixation. He's not sure he could even do it anymore.

"You know," Amy says. "One day I was at work. I had this pounding headache. I was making absolutely nothing and harried as hell. This old guy is watching me and he says, 'Don't worry, you're better than this. I can tell.'"

"Better than this. What did you say?"

"Nothing—I was so surprised I think he meant that I didn't really belong there. That I had more to me than that. The other interpretation isn't so flattering."

"Let's stick with the first one."

"I brought him a brownie sundae on the house. He winked at me. That was worth more than any tip."

THEY START WATCHING a movie, but Dirk is bushed and drifts off in the arm chair half an hour into it. He has a hard time making it through a movie these days. Old and cantankerous. He can feel a hand through his hair and an arm around his neck. The television is on low.

When he wakes up the credits are playing and Amy is nowhere to be seen. He gets up to get a drink of water. At least he has made a friend. He can always use more friends, especially new ones. Purple-headed ones. Yes, he's a cliché—a woman has lightened his mood. But she hasn't saved him—nobody can do that.

The note on the kitchen counter reads:

"UR better than this. Call you soon. Had fun. –A."

Winking smiley face.

Dirk doesn't take it as a criticism. There is potential here, he thinks. But not much, really. He wouldn't bet ten dollars on their future. On his future. On anybody's future. On America's future. On Earth's future.

Sleep comes slowly, but it does come—as if on its own accord. His neighbors are snoring in stereo. He turns the fan on full blast, points it at the wall. He watches the dust spray from the fan blades. He should clean that at some point before he gets black lung.

Right now, he's the dust. Someday he'd like to be the blade. The blade is rotating though, he can see that clearly. It's slow but steady.

REALLY? REALLY?

So I'M GOING to his house because he asked me to, not because I want to, or have any desire to see him really—after everything he did to me, or to be more exact, didn't do *for* me—not that I'm angry or uptight because I'm not. It's just been a long while and I have to sit there and look pretty for him and hide my tats under a blouse or camisole or sashy thing and he gets to sit next to his "girlfriend" who says he *may* become my stepmother, though both terms seem to be pure artifice. It's fine though—I'm going, I'm going. Everything is fine.

In the kitchen, I'm opening drawers and recipe books and trying to figure out what I can bring—and isn't this odd: you are invited over for dinner and you have to fret and worry about what *you* will bring. Courtesy is a beast. I finally decide on fruit salad because it's easy and fresh and who doesn't like easy, fresh fruit? I chop up some pineapple, toss in some blueberries and strawberries and banana and kiwi and grapefruit and a little mango. I would chop up some Granny Smiths, but I'm out of lemon, so I just leave it as is. Except then I realize fruit salad might seem a bit too lazy on my part and I can just see his "girlfriend's" eyes judge me as a lazy, loose, tattoo-hiding potential step-daughter and as a result she may consider bypassing on the marriage thing—although I can clearly think of worse things happening. Not that I've met her or anything—it's just an inkling, because this is how people react and think these days (why I have no idea).

I decide to go to the store to see if I can supplement my fruit salad with something else flashier—that way I can, you know, negate the judging eyes and thoughts and possible consequences as a result of my glaring food-based omission. But just as I'm about to put my flip flops on and flip flop down to the expensive local grocery store with the complicated name, Megan calls and wants to reschedule her drama appointment, which is fine, but when? I have to snap open my day planner and find a day, but rescheduling Megan means doing double-duty some other day—and with French class and guitar lessons and teaching and bartending and my admin stuff plus grading and eating and sleeping and grooming slash bathroom needs and having a "boyfriend" who kind of pays attention to me, plus soccer and working on the house and selling my collectible porcelain dolls on eBay, plus buying some when I can—it could be tough.

"Okay," I tell Megan C. "How about May thirteenth?"

"May thirteenth," she says. "That's two weeks away. I need help now."

"Well, you're asking me to reschedule you, honey. This is what I have."

She sighs and utters a little whimper noise—thirteen-year-olds.

"Fine," she says.

"Fine," I say.

Wow, I think. Really? That's your approach? Really? And when did "Really?" become such a big thing 'cause it wasn't when I was a kid and then suddenly everybody is asking "Really?" and then following that up with a "Just sayin'." Really, really? Or: Reallyreally? It makes no sense. Little does any longer.

I'm about to go out to the store when I realize—since I have my phone in hand—that I have to call Brass Balls, the bar where I work. I realize that if I'm going to meet with Megan that day, I may be late to the bar and "I hope this is okay, but if it's not let me know and I'll reschedule the drama thing," I say. "Cause, you know, I'm committed to you—I just, it's just, I'm juggling a lot of things. Well, you know I am 'cause you can see me, Mr. Brown."

"Yes," Mr. Brown says. We all call him Brownie, but when I want something, I try to be more formal. "Jesus F. Christ. You're like a mouse churning on a wheel. It's exhausting to watch."

I tell him I know that's true—I've always run at full speed until I collapse, and when I collapse, I'm comatose for days, but I tell him that leading up to that I do spin, I do have many activities. This is just the way I am, take me or leave me. It's the way of the world. Type A, etc.

"I can't even sit through a movie, really," I say. Which is true. I fidget. "I mean, wow—who can't do that?" Me, that's who.

So then I'm about to drive on over to the store, but before I do I thought why not check my Facebook and e-mail and blog and website and Instagram and Twitter and Tumblr and Snapchat and Facebook and LinkedIn—though I don't really use that one anymore 'cause who does?—and this has me sending out a few messages, pasting some, copying and pasting, uploading, and just then I realize I forgot to order my French book on cd—the one Forstier told us to get, and which I'm sure I won't understand, but I'll try my hardest, I mean I always do. I also realize I haven't practiced "There She Goes" on guitar, as I'm supposed to, so as I'm ordering the French book on cd, I work on the initial chords of the song. It sounds good. I sound good. Everything will be fine there, I'm sure.

After all of this, I'm a bit tired and then I start thinking, coffee or nap? Coffee or nap? Nap or coffee? Do I rev up and get more done or allow myself some respite for the evening ahead of me? Shit, I think. I forgot about the store. I mean, this is the whole reason I'm up and walking about, I know. And yet, I haven't gone. How is this possible?

So I decide to make some coffee and then I have to decide what kind—I have so many to choose from—Hazelnut and Robust Arabica and French Mission and Jamaican Blue Mountain—and so I decide on the latter because the notion of Jamaica in a cup is fairly pleasing, I have to admit, and I can imagine the scent of parrots and jerk chicken and pineapple emanating from the coffee beans, though by the time I drink it, I don't think this is the case. It's fairly bland.

I'm sitting there drinking my Jamaican coffee thinking why am I so needy? Why am I so intense? Why can't I just go over there like a normal daughter and do the things daughters do—smile and look pretty, and I don't know, darn socks? (Do people still *darn* socks?) Why can't I talk about gardening—day lilies and rhododendrons or oregano? Why can't I hold my own while pushing the envelope forward, conversationally speaking?

But as I'm thinking these things, I'm already mentally cavorting down the aisles of the (very nice) grocery store looking at the cruets and croissants and rutabagas and bok choy and chicken livers and scallops and thinking I don't know what else to get and maybe the fruit salad is enough and maybe I shouldn't be so damn concerned about what my possible future step mother thinks of me anyway, or my father, for that matter, especially my father. He was a good man when he was young, a very good man, a healthy and supportive father and I have zero regrets. And yet. Something lingers at the back of my throat. Like a gag reflex. I'm disconcerted. Perhaps being a father isn't enough. Perhaps children and inevitably disappointing no matter what. I'm sipping my Hawaiian coffee wandering down the grocery store aisle in my mind and fretting about possibilities when I realize I need to actually, you know, get up and do something.

Do what you're thinking—easier said than done. Harness the whirlwind and put it to use. Rein in the thought-stream and refocus it outward. On doing. On action. Do what you're thinking.

I stand up.

I pour the dregs of my coffee down the sink.

I slide on my flip flops.

I think frosted cookies—some kind of bakery good to accompany the fruit salad. Some confectionary to satisfy curiosity, to provide a dessert garnish to whatever dessert *they* provide. Can't lose. Who doesn't like a good cookie?

He will accept it. She will accept it—and perhaps me, at least, for the moment. It will all seem so effortless. When all of this is over tomorrow, I may even be able to settle in for a nap. Maybe. At the store I'll get cookies. Simplify. Lower expectations of myself.

I jingle my keys, open the door, step out of it—one step in front of the other.

THE COLLECTOR

☛

I COLLECT. I collect a lot of things. Of course, there are things I collect and things I don't collect. I *don't* collect napkins. I don't collect antique electronics or bits of scrap metal. I don't collect moldy scraps of bread. This is commonsensical.

I do collect cereal boxes. I have a cereal box room. I devote the room primarily to my collections of Wheaties boxes. This room also contains framed mounted editions of Wheaties boxes, though it mostly contains unopened boxes. My Wheaties collection was appraised at seven grand six hundred and seventeen dollars and eighteen cents. I am proud to say I have one of the largest Wheaties box collections in the U.S.

I collect bricks. I have built a storage shed to house my bricks. Historic bricks can be quite valuable, not to mention aesthetically enriching. Who, for instance, doesn't enjoy "exposed brick"?

Pillows. A room in my house is devoted to softness. Fluff and puff.

Stuffed birds—taxonomical works. These are housed in the basement as the light can quickly damage bird feathers.

Coloring books. Leaves (my collection has five thousand and thirty seven components).

Rare spoons.

Polka albums.

Exotic sewing needles.

All of this may sound mind-numbing. O.C.D. Preposterous. Maybe it is. Fascinating—that's a better word. Things fascinate me. Their scope—their infinite variety. How they offer various takes on the same theme. Their rarity.

The unexpected.

—WOULD YOU TELL her to stop? Shirley.

—What am I doing exactly?

—You know, Ab. If I have to explain it, I'm wasting my breath. I don't like wasting.

Abby blinks at her omelet, which runs toward the right side of her plate. I wouldn't trust it. Marjorie looks at me with that do-something expression.

I don't particularly like interceding, as a fatherly principle. I would prefer to remain on the sidelines. If Marjorie wants an intervention, she still has freedom of will.

Abby cuts into her omelet. She's listening to her sister. Shirley isn't eating. Shirley's on a liquid diet. At five seven and one thirteen she says feels she's too heavy. I don't know.

I eat a hamburger. The "Western." Good mushrooms. We're at a local luncheon. It's nothing special, but a step-up from fast-food. Abby likes fast food. She's accommodating us.

They're arguing because Abby began telling a story. The story happens to revolve around Shirley's tendency toward exhibitionism. Shirley doesn't appreciate a healthy critique.

They squabble over nothing and we let them work it out. That's our parenting style—laissez faire.

Marjorie gives me the goggle-eyes. I think of my Hawaiian shirt collection. Someday I'd like to visit Hawaii. Try a few of them out on the white sand. Or whatever they have there.

In the car I tell Marjorie how odd it seems that we raised these children through the years. Seems so odd in the abstract.

—It is strange. Something from another lifetime.

—I mean, how did we do it?

—How did we survive?

I look at my wristband. It is blotched from sweat. My arm hairs are turning blonde. When we return, Marjorie begins kissing me. I feel dehydrated and soppy.

—It's too hot, I say. You know? Don't you feel gross?

—I'm trying.

This is about the worst thing she could say. We've done therapy. We've lived apart. It's never easy. Nothing is.

—Do you remember that time you went to the...what was it? Flamingo show, maybe? Was that it?

This was in Indiana. Five years ago.

—Yes. Abby bites her lip in the manner of Bill Clinton. We're at her place. I'm watching her goldfish oscillate in their tank. Their tails are the color of Cheetos.

—You were looking for a red flamingo. It was a certain kind of replica. I forget...

—Yes, yes—the Scarlet Ibis.

—Okay, so you remember you let me go off on my own? You said you'd be a while.

—Right, I say.

—That was my first time.

—You mean—

—Yeah. I know, I know. You don't want to know about all this.

—It's okay. We're people. I'm not just your dad. My teeth hit the lemon pulp as I drink the club water.

—There was this man. Floor four—hard to say. He was standing outside of his room, leaning against the door. Just staring. He wore green plaid. I remember that. He was tall and pale. Very skinny—I could see his ribs.

—What did he say to you?

I didn't mean for this to sound accusatory.

—He didn't. I invited myself in. I was sixteen and didn't know any better. I was collecting, too.

—Really? And what were you collecting?

—Experiences. Life.

MY DAUGHTERS don't get it.

Shirley thinks I'm odd. She can't "relate" to my collection of driftwood seagulls. Her concept of fun has more to do with alcohol and finery. Clubbing. A fast beat. The ability to. The desire to. Sexual emancipation.

Abby is younger, more impressionable. She sat on my lap at aged seven as I organized my paint chip collection. I tried to avoid letting her insist. Lead poisoning. However, she has become overwhelmed by my passion. She cannot abide my collection of mysterious gasses. Her interest in helping me date and label has waned. Yet, in her I see a fellow collector. I notice her interest in bookmarks.

However, they also know I am not the sum of my ownership. I am not my pencil collection.

They each live approximately twenty-five minutes away—a healthy distance. Abby and Shirley fail, however, to see eye to eye. Abby is not our natural-born daughter, and we suspect this may have poisoned the well. Didn't have to. Shirley simply can't slash won't understand. She lacks requisite empathy. She has never quite been able to step outside of herself.

COMPETITION. There is only so much time in one day. Only so many things one can do. It's a matter of choice—choosing one thing over another. One person over another. Collecting paint chips, say, is to the exclusion of something else I could collect. This is the way life works. Collecting is, maybe, my attempt to grasp as much as I can.

Marjorie doesn't see the value of all of this. She has me whittle, condense. Organize, label. I've abandoned collections solely to avoid annoying her. She doesn't want to shiatzu my overindulgences.

However, she endures. And I've been faithful—my greatest accomplishment.

My children compete for my attentions—perhaps because they aren't particularly easy to acquire.

Shirley calls. Says she heard I had lunch with Abby.

—I wasn't aware of this. I mean, it's not as if I wanted to be there. I just would have liked to be informed.

—Of what exactly?

—Your plans.

This conversation would never occur with Abby. Shirley has always been the diva, the princess.

—Okay, what would you have me do?

—How about lunch with me about now?

I ARRIVE LATE on purpose.

Shirley is sporting cake makeup and has the A.C. blasting. Icebox. I ask her for a sweatshirt.

—It's summer!

—I'm aware of that. It's just a bit cold in here is all.

She hands me a light paisley scarf. I look at it.

—It's okay. I'll make do.

—I've made soup, she says. I can make you some tea, also.

The soup is gazpacho. The tea is of the iced variety. Shirley says caffeine warms the blood anyway, and that many Arabs drink hot tea to stay cool. So why not cold drinks to warm up?

I'm shivering. Goosebumps. Rubbing my arms.

I eat the gazpacho as Shirley tells me about her shop. Beauty wares. Soaps and oils and lotions and powders. It smells of lilac, always lilac.

She has a cd of songbirds whirring, which is disconcerting given the actual songbirds outside—which I can also hear behind the wall of recorded songbirds. Flute and harp are also involved. She puts more food out—fruit and bread and cheeses. Everything is arrayed nicely.

—Why don't we do this more often? She says.

—We have our lives.

—I mean, without mom.

—We should. But we can also include her. You remember that time we went to the national history museum? We saw the whale exhibit? Those skeletons.

—Of course. I was scared to death.

—You clung to me. You put your feet on my left foot. We walked like that.

—You tried to make me laugh.

—It didn't work. Or at least not much. I cheered you up with a Popsicle outside. You wanted to ride the carousel there. But I didn't....

—You only had change.

—Well, I didn't. I had more. I just didn't want you to get sick. Scared plus sick—no good.

She looks betrayed. She breaks her flatbread in half. She slices cheese. Hands me some.

—Well, it doesn't matter she says. I probably would've gotten sick. My constitution.

—In retrospect, I should've let you go. Things might be different if I had. Let you...It would be calmer.

—Maybe.

She stands. She pours more iced tea. Says she's getting cold, also.

—I think I might turn the air conditioning off.

I don't say anything. I drink my iced tea and listen to my daughter's footsteps.

I RETURN to my collections.

Now that I've entered retirement, I have the time. This can rankle Marjorie if I go overboard. However, it's better this way. If I don't have the time to devote to my collections disorder enters the picture. Then my hobbies become an issue.

There are times when I have to sell. We only have limited space. A few years ago, I found a buyer for my paper fan collection. It was a decent though rather small (227) collection, relatively speaking. I netted two grand. But what I really wanted was additional *space*. This I couldn't acquire easily.

In my will Abby receives the vast majority of my collections. I don't love her more, per se. I do, however, feel she will actually *appreciate* them. Shirley might donate most of my collections to Goodwill. This defeats the purpose forming a collection. They need to be tended to. They are also my children.

Marjorie and I don't have much in common, on paper at least. However, we have our two daughters and she knows how difficult that can be. Once Shirley and Abby left home, our place in the house became questionable. We had to redefine our relationship. The purpose of it.

Now I'm liberated. I'm a father because I wanted to be. I can see them when I want, how I want. I'm not just a tenant and proprietor. It's easier this way.

I love them all. These girls of mine. Perhaps on some level they are a collection in their own right. These women. I'd never say this. I'd never utter it. But I can think it. Nobody can stop that.

We move on step by step.

A HELPING HAND

FOR EIGHT THOUSAND six hundred and fifty two dollars and twenty-two cents (plus shipping), my wife and I bought Gwyneth Paltrow's placenta on eBay (or at least this placenta was *certified* as Gwynie's—though the little Ms. Pacman icon on the bubble wrap did give me pause). This was, seemingly, her Moses placenta, not her Apple placenta. The Apple placenta sold for much *much* more, since it was the equivalent of a rookie baseball card.

Still, I felt fortunate. Eight thousand and change seemed like a bargain for a one-of-one item (especially since we never thought of saving Samantha's placenta). It would have simplified matters if we had.

The purpose of said purchase was to bring a heavy dose of molecular cheer into my wife's body chemistry. She was diagnosed as having PPD, despite our bouncing baby boy. In fact, *because* of our bouncing baby boy, who seemed frankly a bit gimpy and purple to me—though the doctors didn't point to anything specific (despite our fretting questions).

"I don't think I can do it. It's going to be like gnawing on a used tampon," my wife said. "But worse, *much* worse."

She had the shades drawn and the white gardenia and Amazonian water lily scented candles on full fume.

When my wife drew the shades, it always=bad news. Always.

"No," I said. "It will be like *eating* Gwyneth Paltrow's used tampon."

"You're quite the jokester," she said. She had her hands over her eyes. She said she had a headache.

Samantha knew a little about my Gwyneth Paltrow obsession. I watched *Shakespeare in Love* and *Sylvia* on DVD when she was away for work—I even watched her (many) subpar films. I made a scrapbook of her snooty fashion pictures—kept it in the trunk of my car. I still to this day scour her insipid website regularly, base weekly recipes (my wife is none the wiser) upon her celebrity vanity project cookbooks, downloaded all of her self-absorbed songs on I-tunes. There was something about the freckles on the bridge of her nose and the freckles on her left arm and chest and that upturned-nose-look she gave as if she held some surreptitious knowledge about the world and style and class and *society* that you would never know (never even come close to knowing). She was so *choice*. I knew she was a rich, supercilious, actress bitch, and yet she sent me through the roof. I even loved listening to Coldplay, just for the aural proximity to Gwynie.

And I had her intimates in a plastic bag in my freezer. Initially, I had some misconceptions: I thought it might arrive in some kind of special freeze-dried gold-leaf box, but when it arrived it was an ordinary zip lock bag with cold packing around it. I thought she'd mail it vis-a-vis her agency or something, but the return address was Gwynie's pad in London. It could still be fake, but if fake it was a *good* fake.

All day I'd think about her placenta sitting there frozen in my kitchen.

It was an unbelievable turn of events.

As to the pressing question, I have to admit the idea of consuming a part of her body was not unappealing to me. Plus, as I said, it would help with my wife's PPD. Her idea. If bears and squirrels and deer eat their placentas, why not us? Anything for the team.

So, my options were to either have a romantic one-on-one dinner, just Sam and me—sauté Gwynie's placenta with garlic and shallots along with some cauliflower and/or broccoli. Or, invite a bunch of friends over, dish up some kind of placenta casserole. I asked Sam. She shrugged. I decided to go with the group of friends—much easier that way to avoid the subject of what we were eating and why. We could just drink three bottles of cab and gobble up the fricassee without thinking. Which is the direction I decided to go.

The fricassee wasn't all that difficult, really. A little Trader Joe's Thai 7 Spice Seasoning and paprika did the trick, and I added barley for a heartier version. Our friends Bob and Deb brought a nice loaf of sourdough and Carmen made a delicious fruit salad (kiwi, yay!). Our little Nicholas was asleep upstairs in his crib. Sam was effervescent. I wonder if the mere placenta odor helped her mood.

About halfway through the meal, Carmen, in mid bite, inquired about the meat in the dish.

"It has a nice bite, a kind of warm, almost livery taste."

I wanted to lie, but I didn't have it coordinated with Sam at all.

"It's Gwyneth Paltrow," Sam said. Bob placed his fork on his plate, and looked up. I heard that tinkling sound always present at dinner parties. We had a nice Hayden concerto twinkling away in the living room.

"What do you mean it's Gwyneth Paltrow?"

"I have PPD," she said.

"I'm sorry," Cameron said. "But what does that have to do with…"

"Oh, shit," Bob said, realizing.

"The healing power of food," I said.

"You assholes. Were you even planning on telling us—"

"Jesus, I'm going to be sick," Deb said.

"We do have ginger ale," I said. I was just trying to offer a helping hand. "It calms the stomach."

THAT WAS pretty much it.

I thought Bob's comment was a bit over-the-top, a tad melodramatic. But not surprising for him.

Placenta—it's a "thing," I wanted to say. It might be peculiar, but it's still a "thing."

It wasn't as if it was cannibalism, I tried to say. It was a sacred practice in Chinese medicine, at some point, wasn't it? I did some research. The blogs were actually quite supportive of placentophagy—as evidence many cited the real benefits of eating the placenta to the mother. Most offered the theory that the mother only needs to hurdle the social stigma of eating the organ.

After Bob vomited, he told us if we gave him hepatitis or HIV, he would sue us for everything we got. "Got" was his parting word, actually.

It was still Gwyneth Paltrow's placenta, I argued. Academy award winner, man. I tried to make the case that this is A-list celebrity placenta, not just *ordinary* placenta. I also defended the charge of possible hepatitis or HIV.

"Do you really think *Gwyneth Paltrow* would have hepatitis?"

My Gwynie is too pure.

This is when the night got ugly. But it was okay. Zero punches were thrown. No eyes poked out. We may have offended, we may have lost a few valued friends, but life goes on.

WE ALSO had plenty of leftovers.

Usually in our house leftovers tend to sit around and eventually spoil. These leftovers, however, went right away. Sam *loved* the fricassee. Almost *too* much.

"It really does seem to make a difference," she said. "I mean, I feel *energized* somehow." I felt that too.

By the next day the leftovers—and all of Gwynie's placenta—were gone.

By the day after Sam and I were making love again, bonding with our little purple munchkin, everyone happy as clams.

She said "I feel much better. I think it actually was a helping hand."

We didn't even have the runs. Gwyneth Paltrow's placenta seemed to be easily digested. Who knew?

HERE'S THE THING: Sam and I have had our rough patches. We have fought many times. This is normal, but the net effect is that we're a couple who has a history fraught with conflict. I wouldn't normally worry. However, Sam has a memory like a trapdoor. She forgives but she never forgets. She can recall what I said seven and a half years ago—and not only remember what we had for dinner that night, where we were, and what I wore, but also the exact expression on my face. I'm not this way—but I can certainly be short and snipe too easily.

However, this memory works on the plus side as well. After we ate Gwyneth Paltrow's placenta I knew this would be something she would savor, something she would treasure for years. Sam said she *felt* better, and if she felt better I knew she would be fine, and if she was fine I knew that we were fine, and if we *were* fine I knew that everything was fine.

And isn't this the reason we do the things we do? Contentment. We try to improve our lot. I'd do just about anything for that. I have and will.

YOU ARE THE PRODUCT

WHY ARE you here? Strike that—you don't have to answer that. It's what's called a rhetorical question, obvi. Also obvi: you came here for wisdom, for guidance, for that one pint-size nugget of insight which you can squirrel away and unleash upon the world in a huge explosive way. You came here with a plan, a tablet, a book rearing to go. Maybe it's werewolves in space. Maybe it's vampires meets *Das Boot*—*Dracula* in a Submarine. Maybe it's Bambi-grows-up-and-commits-Bambi-patricide. Turns cannibal. Maybe it's *Moby Dick* told through the point of view of a harpoon.

I won't guess.

You're here in the fluorescent buzzing antiseptic room, furnished with cheap mass produced everything because you want to be *humungous*. You want to be naked on the Internet, going viral. Kimmy K times five. Who *doesn't*? You want to be Tom Clancy on PCP. You want to be Neil Gaimon on Ketamine. You want to write a book about Harry Potter's sock drawer. You want readers in Bhutan *and* Tahiti. You want to bathe in money. You want your words organized into a Hollywood mythos.

But we need separation, don't we? We need to see how your Bambi werewolf vampire story is better than slash different than all the rest. Separation. Separation is the jangling key to glorification.

Glorification is the clanking key to mythification. Mythification is the clinking clacking key to historical preservation.

Interlocking—like taut Lego pieces on a Lego battleship.

I'm here to tell you. And you. And *you*…the key to the keys is this: YOU!

You.

Are.

The.

Product. You are the product. Not the story. Not the characters. Not the book. Not the plot. Not even the cover. It's all you all the time.

My entrance into this world—the world that you and I entrance, the world of the word—my entrance was, as you may or not know, Dinosaur erotica. T-Rex orgies. Brontosaurus porn. Sauropod sixty nines. Everything you can imagine we do, dinosaurs did. Minus the lingerie, candles, Barry White and the vases of long stem roses. They went right for the gusto.

This is a domain which took an immense amount of imagination on my part to capture. And research. Before I started I would've thought dinosaur penises were long and sharp, like spears, like tridents. But if I hadn't believed in myself, in my art, I wouldn't be here talking to you today. I had to realize that panting dinosaurs were not the story. The story was—shocking, I know—*me*. The story was the story behind the actual story. I knew dinosaurs because in a distant past life, I was a stegosaurus. You most likely were, also (they were quite common).

But even a good platform is not enough to become humongous. Succeed in your career and parlay that backflow into your writing. But you must, you *must* possess a good platform (former dinosaur, etc.), plus a go-getter mindset. You have to hit the streets. You have to cold call. You have to e-mail your old piano teacher, your cousin's boyfriend's mother's sister. You have to tweet every five minutes. Twitter the shit out of everything. You have to be on Facebook posting about your project's advancement every half-an-hour. Those are the metrics. Make the story of your book the story. Selfie your shit. Show some skin if you need to, pleasure an agent, wear cowboy boots and a pink feathered hat. Hand out post cards at truck stops. Become a spammer. Learn to love the dark web.

Embrace the all!

There is no such thing as overexposure, no such thing as over-doing it. That argument is null and void. Overexposure *is* exposure.

There is also no such thing as bad press. Eat a live jellyfish. Streak through the high school parking lot. Drive your car off a bridge. Juggle black mambas.

As long as they mention your name and your status as an author, you're golden. You. Want. Eyes. On. You.

Of course, I actually didn't begin with dinosaur sex—nobody ever really does. I began writing restrained little stories featuring gauzy muslin and longing gazes and cobblestones and windswept plains. My first book, *Sepia Dreamscape* was, yes, I admit it, self-published (nothing wrong with that!).

But can you imagine the reaction! The horror. The horror!

Yet, were the stories less than worthy as a result? Negative. Were the characters less acutely drawn than the latest *New Yorker* brilliance? Negative. Yet it only sold seventeen copies—and eight of those were to my loving quasi-retired aunt.

At the time I was mousy and introspective and of the mind that my readers should find *me*. Little did I know....

Then I tried my hand at magical realism, fabulism, fantastical whatever-you-want-to-call-it. Talking rocking chairs and television sets that walk the dog and pillows stuffed with the innards of elves. You know, "imaginative." I called the thing *Gesticulations, Reverberations, and Mastications*. "Everything is eating or eaten," I said in my interview with *Rainbow Express*. But the collection only sold forty three copies—seventeen to my loving aunt.

You might ask, why not try a novel? Well, that's what I did.

Nightmare on the Siberian Express was my great Russian work, which counted one thousand five hundred and sixty-seven pages and featured two hundred and eighty-one characters. It took me seven years to write, sold eighty three copies—thirty seven to my loving aunt.

So. Not really a winning strategy.

My marriage collapsed. My health declined. I lost my day job. All in the service of my art.

Fuck art. Repeat after me.

I was in the library researching some kind of Flaubertian minutia on scoliosis for my fourth to-be self-published book when I came across an illustrated best-selling children's book on dinosaurs. Voila, I thought. Just wrench that up a notch and twist it into a curlicue and alter the desired audience.

So I did. New job. Go to the gym five times a week and my doctor says I have the blood pressure of a nineteen year old. And I have a new fiancé, Kirk. Kirk—what a dull jerk.

This isn't complicated, really. You simply go where the readers are. You broadcast your shit with a big-assed megaphone and you ignore the critics—they get *their* books for free.

Well, that's it for me! Thank you for coming to my panel. I hope you found it helpful and encouraging. Keep writing! Keep believing! All that crap.

Please fill out the survey (copies available on the table by the exit). It will take two minutes and you will make the organizer cry tears of joy (promise!). I'll be happy to stay and chat after we conclude. I have all of my books for sale, of course (ha-ha-ha)—as you can see. Of course, I accept Venmo and Paypal.

But don't forget this: Words. They. Don't. Matter. Nobody cares. It's all you. All the time. You.

Hurry Up and Relax: THE EXIT POLL

Use the classic One to Five star rating system to rate the following characteristics of this work of fiction:

___ *Hurry Up and Relax* made me feel better about civilized society and its inhabitants.

___ *Hurry Up and Relax* helped me on the path to become a better-rounded individual.

___ *Hurry Up and Relax* helped my love slash sex life.

___ *Hurry Up and Relax* helped me understand how to give and receive hugs appropriately.

___ Thanks to *Hurry Up and Relax*, I have more friends (or at least acquaintances).

___ Thanks to *Hurry Up and Relax*, I have a more positive body image.

___ Thanks to *Hurry Up and Relax*, I have stopped smoking, vaping, Juuling and taking recreational drugs and am now content to chew on stalks of raw broccoli.

___ *Hurry Up and Relax* gave me a new window into the spiritual world.

___ Thanks to *Hurry Up and Relax*, I now have a sudden desire to attend the ballet, read Tolstoy and learn how to write calligraphy.

___ Thanks to *Hurry up and Relax*, I would like to adopt a large wounded animal and devote my life to its survival.

___ *Hurry Up and Relax* strengthened my belief in the potential of the human life force.

___ *Hurry Up and Relax* made me a better person.

___ *Hurry Up and Relax* initiated feelings of ease and gratification and allowed me to sleep more soundly.

THANK YOU for your time and cooperation! Please text the easily remembered code %O**BVN##(:+)NVJHYT-^UUKUOBCUR@!!!! JNKPO)IEZN?V/R to: 487-7987-759 (HUR-RYUP-RLX) for your free edible slash organic slash biodegradable slash reclining slash realistic stegosaurs figurine. Just add $9.87 for shipping (plus the $19.99 service fee).

ABOUT THE AUTHOR

NATHAN LESLIE's ten books of fiction include *Three Men, Root and Shoot* and *The Tall Tale of Tommy Twice*. Nathan's poetry, fiction, essays and reviews have appeared in hundreds of literary magazines including *Boulevard, Shenandoah* and *North American Review*. Previously Nathan was series editor for *Best of the Web* anthology 2008 and 2009 and he edited fiction for *Pedestal Magazine*. He was also interviews editor at *Prick of the Spindle*. Nathan is the current series editor for *Best Small Fictions* and he is the founder and host of the monthly Reston Readings Series. He teaches in Northern Virginia. Find Nathan on Facebook and Twitter as well as at Nathanleslie.net.